"Oh, my God," Courtney squealed. "Look over there. Look who that is!"

"That's Eric Eastman, the movie star. Didn't you see his last picture? *Murder on My Mind.* It was so scary, and now there he is, putting his handprints in cement. Oh, this is so exciting!"

I tried to focus my camera, but there were a lot of people around him and television cameras, too.

Amidst all the noise and confusion we both heard a distinctive little clunk. Wilheim Von Dog's sunglasses had just slipped off. Courtney bent down to get them, and in one flash, the little dog leaped out of her arms. . . .

Courtney screeched. "Wilheim Von Dog!"

But it was too late. Just as Eric Eastman was placing his famous hands in the wet, sticky cement, Wilheim Von Dog jumped in. . . .

And they all landed on national TV news. . . .

Books by Judi Miller

The Middle of the Sandwich Is the Best Part
My Crazy Cousin Courtney
My Crazy Cousin Courtney Comes Back

Available from MINSTREL Books

COMES BACK

Judi Miller

PUBLISHED BY POCKET BOOKS

New York London Toronto Sydney Tokyo Singapore

A MINSTREL PAPERBACK *ORIGINAL*

A Minstrel Book published by
POCKET BOOKS, a division of Simon & Schuster Inc.
1230 Avenue of the Americas, New York, NY 10020

ISBN: 0-671-88734-3

First Minstrel Books printing December 1994

10 9 8 7 6 5 4 3 2 1

Cover art by Carla Sormanti/Dagwan

Printed in the U.S.A.

For Pat MacDonald, who brought My Crazy Cousin Courtney back

COMES BACK

December 6

Dear Courtney,

I can't believe I'm coming to Beverly Hills for Christmas vacation. I've never been to California. I've never been on a plane. Except for camp, I've never been *anywhere!*

My mom took me shopping and I got a two-piece bathing suit. It's dark purple. I also got a purple notebook to take notes in when we go sightseeing. I just like purple.

I'm trying to picture Christmas without cold, snowy weather, and ice-skating. Do you have a Christmas tree even though it's like summer? Felicity and Dawn are really jealous of me.

I hope you like the Christmas present we got you.

Well, I have to go now. I have to study for a history test tomorrow. I really like seventh grade a lot. Except for math, which is dreadful. But I love English. I've been doing a lot of writing. Wait until you see what I've been writing about!

Love and xxx's,
Cathy

Friday

Dear Cath,

Joan says I can't make a long-distance call, so I'm writing (weird to the max), but I have just a minute. I can't believe you're actually coming. I can't believe you're taking five days off from school to spend more time here. (I can't believe I don't have to go to school, either!) There's this ABSOLUTELY GORGEOUS boy who moved in next door. Well, actually he's half a block away. His name is Gavin and I think he's a tennis pro or something and he's invited me to play. Your bathing suit sounds *super!* We keep the Christmas tree right near the pool. We usually go to Hawaii for vacation, but Bernie needs to sell more houses because of the divorce and Joan has her new dress-designing business to run, but it's just as well because you're coming and that's even better.

We got you a Christmas present, too. I just know you'll love it.

Luv,
Courtney (Tiffany) Alicia Green

P.S. Does your mom like being a people theatrical agent more than an animal agent? Did she get the last fifteen pictures of myself I sent her? If an acting job comes up, tell her to leave a message on our machine, and if the machine is broken to call Bernie, and if Bernie's out, leave a message on his machine. It won't break, it's new.

P.P.S. I almost forgot! Frank will be here. He's coming early, too. He'll be visiting his other grandmother in Los Angeles for Christmas vacation. He says hi!

Chapter One

I had never felt so alone in all my life.

There I was at Los Angeles International Airport in a sea of strangers who were hugging, shouting, jostling, laughing, crying. I clutched my book, *Getting Acquainted with Beverly Hills,* closer to me. I accidentally bumped up against a woman in high heels, a T-shirt, and a mink coat. I said I was sorry. She just glared at me.

I was trying to make my way to the luggage carousel where my crazy cousin Courtney would be waiting for me. I still thought of her as my *crazy* cousin Courtney, even though she had changed when she visited us this past summer in New York. So now I had to learn to call her Courtney without the *crazy*. She had been having problems and acted a little weird because her parents were trying to decide on a divorce, which they finally got, but she was okay now. All that stuff was out of her system and she was into boys big time.

Then I finally spotted her waving to me from across the baggage carousel. But could that be Courtney? She was holding an adorable little fluff-ball of a dog. I knew her mother would never let Courtney have a dog because all their furniture was white. As I got closer I knew it had to be Courtney, though. She was wearing her trademark heart-shaped, red-sequined sunglasses and a T-shirt that said "Beverly Hills Brat." I screamed and she screamed and we ran toward each other. Somehow the little white dog got squished between us and started to yip like a rubber toy being squeezed.

"Meet Wilheim Von Dog," Courtney said, jumping up and down. "Isn't he precious? He's a bee-shawn free-zay. That's how you pronounce it. It's spelled B-I-C-H-O-N F-R-I-S-É with a slanty accent over the *E*. Doesn't it sound like he's a dish of fancy ice cream? He's so adorable." I peered down at it and knew my mom would melt all over this dog who looked like a stuffed animal. He raised his eyes to me, scrutinizing this new person in his life. His nose and paws were charcoal black. Everything else was cloud white.

"Hi, Wilheim Von Dog," I said, shaking one of his little paws. "Pleased to meet you."

"Bernie gave it to me for a present when he moved out." Bernie and Joan were her parents. She called them by their first names because she felt it was good for their egos. She decided it made them feel younger.

Then all at once I noticed a man standing behind her. It must be Bernie, I thought. He was smiling down at me. For some reason I thought Joan would pick me up at the airport.

"Sunday is my day with Bernie," Courtney said, answering my unasked question.

Somehow I had imagined Bernie, who sold houses to movie stars, to look different. I pictured him wearing a checkered suit, smoking cigars, talking out of the side of his mouth. But this Bernie looked like a movie star. He was wearing a floppy cotton hat and a T-shirt that said "Beverly Hills Tennis Club."

I felt slightly dazzled. I expected him to say something like "So this must be Cathy. I've heard so much about you." Instead, he winked and said, "Here's looking at you, kid."

"Frank Sinatra and Johnny Carson belong to the

Beverly Hills Tennis Club," Courtney announced proudly. "The waiting list is a mile long." I wondered if I should write that down in my notebook about my trip to Beverly Hills. So far I hadn't seen anything but the inside of the airport with people dressed like Courtney. Nothing to write about.

Wilheim Von Dog yipped quietly, and I glanced at him. He was wearing a little denim bow that matched Courtney's jeans. Knowing Courtney, she carried the little dog around all the time just like a baby. She loved kids and animals.

"Well, why don't we get some chow," Bernie said after he snatched my suitcase off the carousel. "You must be starving, Cathy."

Courtney hadn't heard him because she couldn't stop chattering about her dog all the way to the parking lot.

"And we have a little doghouse for him with a little burglar alarm."

When we got to the car, I embarrassed myself and gasped. It was so big and beautiful.

"It's a silver Rolls-Royce," Courtney piped up. "Joan got to keep the white one."

I nodded, thinking of the Number 2 subway on the IRT line at home in New York City during a rush hour in a summer heat wave. The Rolls was air-conditioned with a little television and a bar. Courtney and I had glasses of tomato juice.

I kept my eyes focused out the window when we drove into Beverly Hills. Nothing, not even the book on Beverly Hills, had prepared me for this grandeur and lushness. The homes were like mansions. Some of the cars were the length of two cars put together. I had never seen a palm tree before. In New York there were only puny trees except, of course, in Central Park. I never took Courtney to the park because we were too busy getting into trouble when she visited me last summer.

I sat back and relaxed. Nothing like our past adventures would happen in Beverly Hills this Christmas. My crazy cousin Courtney had changed. She was just my cousin Courtney now. What could happen in Beverly Hills? It was so glamorous and sophisticated.

With wide eyes, I watched as we pulled up to a restaurant that looked like a movie set. It was called Chez Beverly Hills.

"A lot of movie stars come here, Cathy," Courtney said. I couldn't speak, just sat there blinking. Maybe I wasn't dressed right. I just had on a blouse and a wraparound skirt, but then that was the way I dressed. Bernie took off his hat and put on a shirt and tie over his T-shirt.

After we went in and my eyes adjusted to the dim lighting, I watched a man shake Bernie's hand

and hand us all huge menus before we were seated. Five violinists clustered around our table and played dreamy music. The only time I'd heard live violin music was in a subway station at home when someone left his violin case on the floor so money could be tossed into it to finance his final year at the Juilliard School of Music.

The menus were pink and gold. I couldn't see over the top of mine. "You girls order anything you want," Bernie said, smiling and peering at us over the tops of his reading glasses. "Cathy, you must be hungry," he said again.

Wilheim Von Dog sat on his own chair with a little bib around his neck, and suddenly I knew that they came here a lot for dinner. Howard, my mom, and I went around the corner to Hung Lo's for Chinese food on Sunday night and Bernie and Courtney went for their treat to Chez Beverly Hills.

I buried myself in my menu. Everything was just so expensive. It was hard for me not to be shocked by the price, because before my mom married Howard, we had always been so poor. Nothing prepared me for these prices.

"I'll have a steak medium rare with hot mustard and grilled tomatoes, and I'll share it with Wilheim Von Dog," Courtney said. Courtney had weird eating habits.

I suddenly felt shy about ordering. I always ordered the least expensive thing on the menu, but I didn't want to do that now because Bernie might be hurt. I didn't want to get anything I could spill. I wanted something I could eat quietly. Finally I decided on the french-fried shrimp. They were crunchy and could be noisy, but I decided I really couldn't make a mistake eating them. I had to fight to keep my upper eyelids open. I was tired and hungry. There was a three-hour time difference between New York and California, and it was way past my dinnertime.

It had been like no other day in my life.

I had never been on a plane.

I had never been outside New York except to camp.

I had never seen a palm tree.

Bernie dropped us off in front of a huge house up a winding driveway. "What are you doing living in the public library?" I said drowsily to Courtney.

I don't know how I got there, but all at once I was standing in front of a massive wooden door with a huge brass knocker. Above the knocker were a Christmas wreath and a picture of Rudolph the Red-Nosed Reindeer that Courtney had obviously drawn sometime in the fourth grade. The nose was bright red. As Bernie drove away, the door opened and a lady who could have been my mom's twin opened the door.

Chapter Two

"You must be Cathy," she said and hugged me.

She wasn't anything like I expected. The only time I met her was when I was five at somebody or other's wedding. I didn't remember her at all. She and my mom are first cousins, which makes Courtney and me second cousins, I guess. Well, cousins, anyway. My mom and Joan were close as kids, but moved away and lost touch.

She wore a long, red quilted robe and in addition to looking like my mom resembled Courtney a lot but taller. Joan gave me a quick tour of the house. I had just never seen anything like it. The living room was sunken and everything in it was white and beige except for the coffee table and the end tables, which were glass and gold.

In the kitchen Courtney was spooning vanilla Häagen-Dazs ice cream into Wilheim Von Dog's little dish. I glanced at the clock and saw that it was nine o'clock, so that meant it was midnight New York time. The only night I was allowed to stay up until midnight was New Year's Eve and then I usually fell asleep instantly after the giant glowing red apple dropped in Times Square ushering in the new year.

"You must be exhausted," Joan said after a while. "We have plenty of bedrooms." She flung her arms wide as if the house were the Beverly Hills Hilton. "But Courtney said you'd want to sleep in the same room so you could talk."

Talk? It was all I could do to keep from yawning and falling asleep on my feet all the time. I could see Courtney outdoors near the shimmering, midnight-colored pool where the glittering gold-and-silver Christmas tree was. She was putting Wilheim Von Dog to bed. Poor kid. Bernie and Joan had actually gone through with their divorce. Wilheim Von Dog must be helping her through this hard time. I vowed to be super nice to her while I was in Beverly Hills. My eyelids fell closed then, and I just wanted to go to bed. I was too tired to unpack and felt okay about it. After all, Courtney didn't unpack for almost two whole months last summer. And then she did it just before she went home.

Joan showed me to our room, and I was undressed and under the covers before Courtney even came back. I had a dream that night that the alarm went off and someone tried to steal Wilheim Von Dog, but our friend Frank was there and leaped over the Christmas tree, caught the doggie napper and rescued the quivering Wilheim Von Dog.

I sat straight up in bed in the middle of the night when I heard it.

POP! And another *POP!*

"Are you awake, Cathy?" Courtney asked in her innocent voice, popping her ever-present bubble gum.

I wondered how long she had let me sleep.

"No," I replied grumpily.

"Are you mad at me for waking you up?" she persisted in her little kid voice.

I remembered then the lovable side of Courtney. She had the ability to make people mad at her and then make them unmad at her almost instantly.

"Why should I be mad at you?" I asked crisply, trying to sound mad because I really should have been.

"Well, I just woke you up out of a sound sleep," she answered, not getting my sarcasm.

"Courtney," I said, deliberately not hearing her. "It's three o'clock in the morning."

California time.

"There's this guy, Cath," Courtney said with a loud pop.

I couldn't stand it. Was this boyfriend number three?

"He's a little older," she said, handing me a piece of bubble gum.

How could she have three boyfriends? It wasn't fair. I didn't even have one. Our friend, Frank, who she met with me in New York, was crazy about her. Her tennis pro hunk, Gavin, liked her, and now another one? I bet he was sixteen or even eighteen. I wouldn't put it past her.

"This isn't Gavin you're talking about?" I asked, double-checking.

"The hunk? No, this one's a *little* older."

"How *old,* Courtney," I finally said.

"About a hundred years old."

I nodded. That explained it. She *was* crazy still!

"Let's get some sleep," I said.

"Wait, Cathy, see there's a rumor going around Beverly Hills that there's this old man who's being held near here against his will, and I think he needs saving."

Just then I saw a triangle of light and a crimson bathrobe appear in it. "Girls," Joan said, leaving the door ajar. "It's after three in the morning. You can do all your catching up tomorrow."

The door closed and I was reminded of my mom doing the same thing to us when Courtney was in New York. My mind calculated slowly that it was a little after six in the morning New York time. In New York the people who baked bread and bagels and doughnuts would be delivering them to delis and restaurants. Joggers would be appearing in the winter sunrise. My mom and Howard would be fast asleep waiting for their alarm to buzz, safe in the knowledge that I was in Beverly Hills and being taken care of.

"I think we should let the little old man be. Someone else can save him if he needs rescuing," I said. "Let's get some sleep."

"Cathy, where's your Christmas spirit? Just because we have tropical weather doesn't mean there's no Santa. I say we have to free him."

I shut my eyes.

She was doing it again.

Bribing me with a charitable cause. She wanted me to help some poor unfortunate soul. And all she'd told me so far was that there was a *rumor* he was being held.

"Can't we talk about this tomorrow morning?" I asked, knowing somehow I was going to lose.

"Oh, no, we have to save him tonight. It would never work in daylight," Courtney said emphatically.

I nodded.

Of course, I should have known. My crazy cousin Courtney was even crazier surrounded by palm trees and boyfriends.

"I've picked out our clothes," Courtney said in a low, almost menacing whisper.

What! I wanted to yell at her. Had she totally flipped? She expected us to go out and search for a *rumor?*

The clothes she picked were all black, turtleneck tops and black stirrup pants. Then I noticed something on top of her pink-and-white vanity table. For a moment fear stuck in my throat—I thought they were guns. They turned out to be flashlights.

"Courtney," I whispered. "All we need are masks to look like cat burglars."

"Shhh," she hissed.

"You know it's almost six-thirty in the morning New York time?"

"Shhh."

We crept down the white-carpeted steps being careful to avoid the creaks and stole out into the backyard.

"Our estate ends on the far right-hand side," she said. "We can just keep walking."

Estate?

We walked at a spritely pace. How did she know where to go? I should have asked myself. All at once we heard a mournful, wailing noise, and I stopped cold.

"Courtney," I said. "Don't play around. This is scary enough as it is."

She kept on walking and I followed along.

"That wasn't me."

"Maybe we should turn back," I said. "By the way, where are we going? How do you know where this man is?"

"Cathy, think about a poor old man. That moaning may be from *him*. Maybe he's like that other poor old man who was locked in that attic for years and grew a long white beard in *A Tale of Two Cities*.

I was stunned. Courtney had read a book—and one by Dickens?

As if reading my mind, she said, "I saw it on the late show."

Then I heard another moan, a long, low cry of despair like that of a coyote in the desert. Had the hundred-year-old man heard us and was he now calling to us to rescue him?

Trembling, Courtney and I hugged each other in the moonlight. I knew then it was too late to go back. Courtney was going on, no matter what, and I couldn't desert her. As my mom would have said—finish what you've started. I squeezed my eyes shut.

It would be better if I didn't think about my mom as we trudged forward.

Finally we stopped in front of a dilapidated old house. Moss and ivy were growing all over it. Even the palm trees in the front yard were ancient and sickly, sticklike. I wondered if the old house really was deserted.

Courtney had taken off, leaving me as she headed for the back of the house.

Catching up to her, I said, "You've been here before, haven't you?"

"Yep."

"But you've never been inside?"

"Nope."

"How come?"

"I was waiting for you."

Chapter Three

"All you have to do is lift that doohickey," Courtney whispered.

I peeked through the door at the doohickey. It was an old-fashioned screen door with a tiny hook. The doohickey I guessed was the tiny hook and was holding the door closed from the inside.

"What you need to do," she said like a professional thief, "is slip a credit card between the doorframe and lift up on the doohickey. The door should open then."

We heard another moaning sound and we froze. Slowly I turned to scan the backyard. The moon was full, hanging like a heavy yellow ball in the dark sky. There were no stars. The shadowy backyard became even more menacing, and I wanted to leave, to go anyplace but where we were. When I turned back, I saw Courtney with a credit card, which she was using to lift the doohickey—I mean hook—up.

"Courtney, where did you get that credit card," I hissed.

"It's mine," she whispered. "Shhh. I almost have it."

I peeked into the darkness behind us once again. I thought of New York City, where it might be snowing and safe. People would be going shopping later that day at Macy's. Little kids would sit on Santa's lap and recite their Christmas lists. My mom and Howard would be home still, drinking coffee and waking up. I liked Howard. True, he wasn't my father, but my father wasn't around and Howard had married my mom.

I would hate to lose Mom and him when Courtney and I got murdered.

"Trust me," I heard Courtney say when I noticed her looking at the tears rolling down my cheeks. She sneaked in through the now-open door. I hesitated before ducking my head and following. I remembered Courtney saying—where's your Christmas spirit? I had to help if I could. No one could challenge my Christmas spirit. Once my Girl Scout troop went into an inner-city neighborhood and put on a show. Once I wrote an essay on the true meaning of Christmas and got an A plus.

So off I went, following my crazy cousin. Courtney moved slowly in the darkness ahead. She waved her flashlight in broad circles, scanning the area ahead of her. Maybe there really was a poor old guy in the house. Maybe he was tied up. Maybe in the cellar. I hoped not. That would be too scary. The heck with Christmas spirit.

"Down, Cathy," Courtney whispered urgently. I understood that that would make us less visible. At the same time it occurred to me that we had actually broken into someone else's home—whose, I had no idea. I felt very shaky as I crawled slowly behind Courtney, my flashlight in my mouth. Ghostlike figures rose up on all sides of me. I felt terror bubble up in my throat, and I almost screamed until I realized the ghosts were furniture covered in white sheets—well, dirty white sheets.

When we crawled to the center of what I guessed was the living room, we stopped and shone our flashlights along the walls. They were covered with weird posters of people with faces as white as sheets. They were really eerie. Some of them had purple lips and wore capes. Everything had been silent for the past few minutes. Then we heard the moaning wail rise once more, and we crashed into each other as we frantically turned in circles and scurried behind the nearest sofa. We had really done it this time, I thought. Now it was definitely too late to turn back.

But where was the wailing coming from? Was it a poor, little old man? We didn't have long to wait for our answer.

All at once the lights flashed on, and a little gray-haired man leaped into the room from the front hallway. Both man and house were worn and tattered around the edges.

"Who's there?" he said. "Come out or I'll sic my attack dog on you." A pathetic old dog sagged to the floor next to him and collapsed.

Courtney and I stood up and she brushed herself off. One thing about my crazy cousin Courtney, she always looks good in any situation.

This was our chance to save him if this was the man who needed saving. Courtney sucked in her breath. I held mine. We had broken into this poor man's house.

"We've come to save you," Courtney said, doing an imitation of Joan of Arc. Actually her acting was getting better and better. "I've heard a rumor that you're being held here against your will. But we can bring you canned foods, soup and sauerkraut, and even a Christmas tree if you want."

The little old man stared down at his attack dog, who was lounging on top of his owner's feet scratching fleas. And then he laughed. I didn't see what struck him so funny, but he laughed and he kept on laughing. He was clutching a sheet covering a chair. The sheet slipped and the man fell to the floor. We had to help him back up. Then I got worried because he started to wheeze as he dried his eyes with a corner of the sheet.

"That's the funniest thing I've ever heard," he said after catching his breath. "That beats the time Wanda Lovelace walked onto the set in a gorilla costume eating a banana. Well, that was long before your time. Do you girls go to school?" he asked, regaining his composure. He did sputter a bit as he spoke, the way people do when they're trying not to laugh.

"Yes, sir." I said. That was usually the lead-in question for getting into a lot of trouble.

"I go to school in New York City," I said.

"Ah, yes, New York. I was there the day they opened Radio City Music Hall. Over sixty years ago. How time flies. And you?"

"Beverly Hills Junior High."

I'd never met anyone so old.

"Well, obviously they didn't teach you not to break into people's houses. You see, I am the caretaker for the estate of Tyrone Stroheim." He stood a little taller then but was still short and still wheezing. "Mr. Stroheim was the greatest movie director in silent films. This is a silent film museum."

That explained the posters. Actually the people did look like the silent film stars I'd seen on a program on public television. I don't think they had good makeup artists then.

"For the last sixty years I have been waiting for someone to buy this museum, but so far no takers. I'm still waiting. I just had an idea. Maybe I could hold you captive and make a lot of money."

Courtney had turned around and was inching slowly away, along the wall toward a little red box. I could tell she was terrified. My eyes must have resembled large round marbles. Then I heard an ear-splitting sound from an alarm. Courtney must have set off the burglar alarm. The little man stuck his fingers in his ears and murmured, "Oh, no, no." The dog leaped up but didn't have the energy to do anything and had nowhere to go, so he sat back down. The Beverly Hills cops would be there in no time, I thought. I glanced over at Courtney, who was facing the wall. She turned then and bit her lips to make them appear redder and finger-combed her curls. This would make a nice little headline: GIRLS WITH CHRISTMAS SPIRIT TRY TO SAVE SCROOGE. In fact, Courtney didn't have to say what she usually said. "Courtney Green, no *e* at the end, from Beverly, like the girl's name, Hills, California." The police probably knew her name and all.

"I guess we touched off the burglar alarm," Courtney said sweetly to the man.

I was staring right at a little brass plaque that said THE MUSEUM FOR SILENT FILMS, 1925, while she went into her sweetness act.

"No." The small man was wheezing again. "Actually no, it's worse. When you turned around and started groping the wall, you pushed up the little lever on the other."

A white statue with no arms almost toppled when Courtney moved backward and bumped into it. I guess she was trying to hide from embarrassment and shame.

"That's the fire alarm, I know. The fire fighters don't usually knock when they come—they just rush in with hoses. It happened in 1954 when I left my pipe in the ashtray. There was one burning ember that turned into a fire. I almost lost the whole collection of silent films, depriving the world of its silent heritage. Of course I've quit smoking since then. But we can't call and tell them to turn around."

"Why not?" Courtney asked.

I covered my face with my hands, knowing I didn't want to hear the answer.

The dog got up on his four legs, moaned, and wailed in competition with the alarm, then shivered before he sank down again. At least that was one question answered. The moaning we'd heard before came from the dog, not any human.

"I have no phone," he answered. "I couldn't hear

it ring a lot of the time anyway. My hearing's not what it was. Today I can hear pretty good. Good enough to hear the alarm, but I know it must be louder for you. I felt it was bonging inside my brain. We have to get the collection from the cellar out into the yard before they come!"

The cellar. Why? I wondered. Courtney answered my why in a minute. She raised herself to her full height standing up very straight. This is a good deed. This is our mission. "C'mon, Cathy!" she yelled and followed the man to the cellar. Then we saw them. Stacks and stacks of reels of film. Everything that belonged to the Museum for Silent Films. If we didn't work fast, all these films could accidentally be ruined by the water the fire fighters shoot everywhere. We couldn't let that happen.

"To the yard!" Courtney shouted with armfuls of film.

The caretaker gazed at her sharply and said, "Just carry the reels up and be silent. And remember, I'm not letting you girls off the hook yet."

I knew I was crying. This wasn't what I had thought I'd be doing in Beverly Hills. It had seemed so glamorous in *Getting Acquainted with Beverly Hills*. It didn't say anything about a Museum for Silent Films or a little old man who probably hadn't spoken to anyone for fifty years and a dog that moaned and howled and should have been walked forty years earlier. Let's face it, I was overtired. And when I get overtired, I get, like my mom says, cranky.

I heard Courtney say over the sirens, "That's about it, sir." The clanging of the fire department surrounding the house was intense.

We walked out of the house with our hands up, and it took some time for the firefighters to hear over the shouting and the clanging that it really was only a false alarm.

Why Courtney was explaining to the fire department about backing into the white statue without arms, I'll never know. But then the fire fighters wanted to know why she was backing away. She explained that she was scared of all the noise from the alarm. At this point the curator recovered from his attack of shyness, which resulted from seeing more people than he had in the last thirty years, and explained that the girls had broken into his museum.

"The museum?" one firefighter asked. "But this is a residential area."

"Well, it's the Museum for Silent Films. I'm waiting to sell it. It's the estate of Tyrone Stroheim, the greatest silent film director who ever lived."

"But why did you break into the museum?" the fire fighter persisted. I was sure the Beverly Hills cops would be there in two minutes.

"We broke in to save this man and bring him cans of sauerkraut," Courtney said.

I put my hands over my eyes.

"Shouldn't you kids be home in bed? Isn't it Christmas vacation? Don't you want to go to Disneyland? Don't you have boyfriends?" the fire fighter asked.

I shut my eyes then and was sorry when I opened them. A flash went off in my face. Sure enough the police had come and with them the reporters.

We were finally let go after we called Joan, who drove over to claim us, crying and embracing us both. She had to promise to keep us out of trouble. Bernie pulled up right behind her in the other Rolls-Royce, and I could see he was trying hard not to laugh.

The caretaker dropped all charges against us because a very good-looking man approached and said, "I'd like to buy this museum of yours. I'd like to live in it and renovate it." It turned out he was a Hollywood director and admired the films of Stroheim.

I looked around dizzily. It was all happening again. The three-ring circus that was my Crazy Cousin Courtney. Well, at least this time it happened in Beverly Hills, and my mom knew nothing about it. It was around ten A.M. in New York (I wondered when I'd stop figuring time in New York hours), and she was at work. She had no idea that I hadn't slept all night and that we had broken into a silent film museum, almost getting the place flooded, and then got it sold.

At least I could be safe in the knowledge that she knew nothing.

Chapter Four

If I'd been keeping a journal of my Christmas vacation in Beverly Hills, I would have written—"Day One. I slept."

I had never slept all day before except when I had the flu. I woke up only briefly to hear Courtney on the phone.

"I'm sorry, Bernie, but if it wasn't for us, that museum would have never been sold. Don't I deserve some kind of commission? Yes, I know the caretaker can retire now and go to Shady Pines Rest Home and that's a reward, but—"

I could just picture Bernie laughing again.

But I wasn't.

I just rolled over and went back to sleep again. Until about three in the afternoon, which was six o'clock New York time. I heard Joan calling to tell me I had a phone call. My mom. I reached over and lifted the receiver.

"Mom?"

Courtney was curled up like a cat on her bed casually listening to my conversation. Wilheim Von Dog was in our room lapping up Häagen-Dazs ice cream from his little bowl that said "Dog."

I shot Courtney a look that should have made her turn away. I was, well, cranky. The look did nothing to move Courtney.

"No, Mom, I'm okay. Oh, Joan told you all about it. It was in the papers, all the way in New York? Well, see, we just wanted to save this poor old man, bring him cans of sauerkraut and stuff.

"No, I know I'm their guest. Yes, I know Courtney is responsible for me." Then I realized what I was saying. Courtney was totally irresponsible. She had brought me down to her level. I, who had always been this good kid. Well, that was before she came into my life, anyway.

"How's your new zoo shaping up, Mom? Oh, great, you got an orangutan. And a gorilla that sings?" My mom had decided to try being an agent for animals again. Suddenly I felt homesick.

"No, Mom, I'm not trying to change the subject. Maybe we can go sightseeing or to the movies or—" Then I stopped myself. I hadn't seen enough of Beverly Hills to know *what* we could do. All we had done was get into trouble, and we could go back to New York to do that.

"Okay, bye, Mom. I love you, too."

She hung up.

I rolled over and slept until dinner. During dinner I stayed silent except to say things like—Pass the salt. Would you like the potatoes? No, I'm full.

"Are you okay, Cath?" Courtney asked.

"Sure," I said, my lips tight.

"Could you pass the corn?" she asked, acting like a saint.

Some halo.

"Sure," I said.

I then watched her scrape off all the kernels of corn from a cob and stir them in with her mashed potatoes and then the whole thing in gravy. It's funny that so much of her was so sophisticated and the rest was like a little kid. But I was no better.

I mean, I trusted her, hadn't I?

Believe it or not, after sleeping for a whole day, we fell into bed and slept the whole night, too. Courtney fell asleep, popping and chewing midbubble. Well, at least she didn't chew in her sleep.

* * *

The next morning when I woke up, I felt terrific. Courtney was still sleeping facedown. Wilheim Von Dog was facedown on his little pillow, too. I figured out that he must spend one out of seven nights in his burglar-alarmed, air-conditioned doghouse. I put on my new two-piece purple bathing suit and threw a white smock over it. Then I grabbed my purple notebook that matched. It was a whole new day and there was no telling what I might write in it. We might even go sightseeing.

Joan was downstairs sitting at the table, and Bernice, the maid, who called Courtney "Miss," was serving bacon and eggs and croissants. Everything smelled yummy. Outside through the glass doors I could see the sun casting gold and silver dots on the pool like pebbles skimming a lake.

"Have a seat, dear," Joan said.

I watched as a blob of creamy scrambled eggs and two pieces of crispy bacon slid onto my plate. Joan carefully placed a croissant on a little dish for me and lined up a jar of jelly, a jar of marmalade, and a crock of butter in front of me like pieces in a chess game.

"Now," she said, "you and I can have a nice little chat."

I couldn't imagine what about. I had just met her.

I nodded.

"What did you do to Courtney last summer to change her so?"

A tiny piece of bacon slid out of my mouth.

This was a *changed* Courtney? This was the same old Courtney. I found myself straining to imagine what she must have been like before she came to New York.

Impossible was the only word I could come up with.

"Well," I said, searching for just the right words. I had always been good with words, hadn't I? "When Courtney came to New York last summer, we just gave her some chores and a job at Camp Acorn. She got a chance to be more, uh, thoughtful."

I could never tell a lie. That part was true. Courtney was basically a good kid when she was at her best. Of course, she hadn't been at her best lately.

I raised my head as two other people wandered into the room and sat down at the table to eat breakfast. Joan introduced them to me.

"This is Enrico Forico," she said. "The most fabulous designer in all of Beverly Hills."

Enrico Forico nodded in agreement, then reached over, picked up my hand, and kissed it. No one had ever kissed my hand before. I noticed little swatches of fabric pinned to his shirt as he mumbled, "Tent green. It will take Beverly Hills by storm, darling. But just a splash of hot pink like a kiss on an olive. Everyone will suddenly want to be dressed like a tent."

Joan smiled. "Enrico is my partner," she said. "We call it Joanrico."

"And this is Shirley, our publicist," Joan said. I studied this very short woman with very bright pinkish-orangey hair who was nibbling a croissant. She winked at me. She was wearing a long strand of pearls and was dressed all in black.

"Well, I'm late to work," she said and walked into the living room, where she picked up a phone and never took it off her shoulder. In fact she filed her nails while she talked. I know, I kept peeking.

Meanwhile Enrico and Joan had finished breakfast and gone into the living room. They were holding hands and jumping up and down. I watched the glass-and-gold end tables shake.

"I love it, I love it!" Enrico sang over and over. "All of Beverly Hills will be rushing to buy tent-drab green with just a smidgen of wild pink, just a smidgen. Not too much—that is where the artistry is. Think tent. Think green!"

Suddenly I felt dizzy.

As I studied the whole scene, I was reminded of Phyllis's Zoo before the property she was renting was condemned. Parakeets chirped in time to the typewriter. Ginger the piglet, the office mascot, had sat oinking away in her wastebasket. My mom wheeled and dealed. Who knew who or what you'd find in her office? Now she was setting up Phyllis's New Zoo.

I needed fresh air and wandered back into the kitchen. Opening the glass doors, I could see that the sun was reflecting on the pool so that it was like blue and green chips of cut glass. The colors of Courtney's eyes. I had a freshly sharpened pencil. I was eager to begin writing. But where to start? Maybe! "My Crazy Cousin Courtney Comes Back."

Because even though I was here and she used to be there, she was definitely back in my life. So *back* it was.

Then I jumped. Courtney had suddenly materialized behind me. She had a habit of doing that. She was wearing a blazing, splashy bikini of orange and yellow polka dots on a red background. Wilheim Von Dog had a perky little bow to match.

She made a sweeping theatrical circle and plopped down on a chaise lounge on the other side of the pool, face to the sun, arms out.

I kept on writing.

Chapter Five

Finally Courtney lowered her heart-shaped, red-sequined sunglasses and asked innocently, "Cathy, are you mad at me?"

What could I say? I was her guest.

"Because in the end, the little old man got everything he wanted except the cans of sauerkraut.

"And he didn't press charges."

I could tell she was waiting for me to say something. Courtney always said I let my emotions glob up until they turned to stale pieces of bubble gum and gummed up the works.

Suddenly I said, "Remember when you pulled on

that little red handle and set off the fire alarm, and we thought we were going to be locked up forever in the Beverly Hills police station?"

Courtney started to laugh. There was something about Courtney's laugh that always made everyone feel good. It was infectious.

"And the attack dog?" She giggled. "He looked more like a rag doll. But could he wail and moan."

We both howled and screeched.

I could barely breathe, I was laughing so hard.

"But the funniest thing, Courtney, was when we walked out and the firefighters couldn't get your story straight."

Courtney had turned facedown pounding the edge of the chaise lounge. I was sitting cross-legged, tears rolling down my cheeks.

So it was hard to hear Joan when she came and stood by the pool saying, "Girls, Frank is here."

My heart flipped over in the split second that I looked up. He seemed to be standing right where the sun was strongest, and the first thing I saw was that sandy lock of hair that fell across his forehead so adorably.

Then I noticed his golden-tan arms with their light blond hairs. How could he be tan in the winter in Idaho? I wondered. He was wearing a white shirt rolled up to the elbows and khaki pants. His amber eyes were hidden by sunglasses. I uncrossed my legs and became entirely speechless.

The very thing that I didn't want to happen had happened.

Four months after I last saw him I was still hopelessly in love with the boy my cousin Courtney liked.

"Hi, Frank," Courtney said, waving to him.

Is that all? Somehow I expected her to rush up and hug him or something. Did she feel embarrassed because I was there? My crazy cousin Courtney? Was she being careful not to hurt my feelings because she got him and I didn't? (Courtney was basically a good kid.)

Frank walked along the pool and sat down on a chaise lounge. There was something different about him, but I couldn't put my finger on it. Had he grown taller? He hadn't put on any weight. He somehow seemed less stiff and shy than he had been the summer before when we had all hung out together in New York.

Frank was almost fifteen, so he was a whole year older. But he was from Idaho, so that made him seem younger. That was one of the reasons I liked him.

Then I heard a shout.

"Hey, gorgeous!"

"Hey, Gavin!" Courtney shouted back.

I could see a boy holding a tennis racket through the chain-link fence behind the pool. Standing beside him was another guy, tall with black curls, carrying a guitar.

Then before I knew it, Courtney had jumped up and let them into the pool. We had a whole party and everyone was saying, "Hi."

"This is my neighbor, Gavin." She waited a beat. "He's a tennis pro. Or almost."

Gavin was everything she said he'd be. A true hunk. He was tall with wall-to-wall muscles, light brown curly hair. He could have been a movie star, but still he was no Frank. I was surprised Courtney couldn't see that.

He introduced the boy with the guitar. "This is Rock," he said. "He's from Liverpool, England. He's trying to make it as a rock star, and he's our part-time gardener." Then he punched Rock, and Rock punched him back, his twinkling periwinkle blue eyes shining. "I'm his bodyguard," Rock said.

I liked his accent. I was too shy but I wanted to tell him we had done a map of Great Britain in geography with colored pins and I knew exactly where Liverpool was. It was the red pin.

"And this is my cousin, Cathy, from New York," Courtney said. "She's visiting us for the Christmas holidays."

"Oh, is that right?" Rock said. "Hey, man, I want to go to New York someday. That's where all the action is."

There was a long silence.

I heard my voice say, "And this is Frank. He's from Idaho. He's visiting his grandmother for the Christmas holidays."

"Hi, Frank," Rock said. "Welcome to BH. Beverly Hills."

I found myself liking Rock. In a way he reminded me of Courtney. Energetic and enthusiastic and friendly.

And then no one said anything for a while. The silence became more and more awkward. It occurred to me that no one knew what to say.

Suddenly I saw that Courtney had jumped into the pool. Her hair, a natural strawberry blond, was coppery when wet and her long lashes were matted like midnight lace. Everyone thought Courtney wore a lot of eye makeup, but I knew, for a fact, that she wore only a dab of green eyeshadow to match her eyes and Pistachio Pink nail polish. Every once in a while she wore a slash of juicy orange lipstick but never anything more.

Every boy had his eyes on my cousin Courtney as she dived in and out of the rippling water in her bright, splashy bikini like a human dolphin.

Then I realized something.

Courtney was an excellent swimmer.

Last summer one of her escapades had been to fall into the New York Aquarium and have to be rescued waving goodbye to the dolphins. Of course, she got her name in the paper, but they spelled it wrong.

Now here she was stepping out to the end of the diving board. We all held our breaths. Then, like a yellow-and-orange streak, folding herself up, she jackknifed and landed in the pool perfectly with hardly any splash.

No one said anything.

Then I heard Frank say, "Cathy?" and I nearly jumped.

"Huh?"

"Would you like to take a walk?"

"Where?" I asked. I mean it was nice of him to ask me, but it was Beverly Hills. Nobody walked. Everybody drove.

"Well, down the driveway," he said. I could see his point. The driveway was about two city blocks long. I figured he had probably had a fight with Courtney and wanted to talk to me about it.

"Sure," I said, slipping on my white smock.

"How was your trip?" Frank asked.

"My trip?"

"Yes."

"Well, uh, it was long."

"Oh, I know what you mean. We had a stopover in San Francisco, and that took a really long time."

"I've never been to San Francisco," I said. Then I wondered how my cousin Courtney, who was playing dolphin, would have handled this. She was so good with boys.

But this was the wrong boy for me.

This was Courtney's boyfriend.

CHAPTER SIX

"Girls!" Joan said, opening our bedroom door the next morning. "Bernie just called. He has some extra time, and he wants to take you sightseeing!"

"Super!" Courtney said, springing out of bed.

"Don't forget to have breakfast or you'll get hungry," Joan said.

Courtney grabbed Wilheim Von Dog, after grabbing some Oreo cookies smeared with chunky peanut butter, her favorite rush breakfast. We were out the door just as Bernie was pulling up in the silver Rolls. He was wearing his same hat that looked like a crushed artichoke and a T-shirt that said "Disneyland."

We climbed into the backseat.

"Where to, Daddy?" Courtney chirped and I heard the slip. I thought she always called him Bernie.

"Anywhere you want, Princess. I'm taking the day off." I did notice there was a car phone, and he had a beeper on the dashboard.

"Cathy, is there anything special you wanted to see?" he asked.

I wanted to say everything, but I felt tongue-tied. I managed to say, "Wherever you take us will be fine. I've never been to California."

I had the Instamatic Howard had given me for my early Christmas present, and I had my notebook. I was making a mental note to design a special scrapbook called *Beverly Hills Christmas* and put all my snapshots in it and do the lettering in blue and red or possibly green and red.

We drove down Sunset Boulevard as Bernie explained that Los Angeles was called "The City of Angels." I made a careful note and snapped pictures. Then we went to the Farmers' Market with its row upon row of freshly picked California fruit and vegetables. Bernie bought us sacks of oranges and grapefruits, and Courtney peeled an orange and fed one to Wilheim Von Dog. Then we went to Chinatown and walked around and then we visited Little Tokyo and had sushi at a sushi bar. At Griffith Park, high in the hills above the city, we watched people horseback riding, playing tennis, picnicking, and hiking. I thought of New York again and wondered if it was snowing there.

Then the best part. We went up to the Griffith Observatory and Planetarium and I got a lot of good pictures. I kept loading my camera. Courtney and Wilheim Von Dog would probably be in the background of each picture since Courtney kept stepping in front of the camera.

"The museum, kids?" Bernie asked

Courtney groaned. She had seen the museum before, but I wanted to go. I love museums. We went to the La Brea Tar Pits to examine the fossils of prehistoric saber-toothed tigers, mastodons, and giant vultures that had sunk into the pits more than 35,000 years ago. I wondered what my mom could have done for their careers if they were still alive and roaming New York City.

I could see Courtney was starting to get restless. Obviously there was somewhere else she wanted to go.

"Honestly," she said very loud in her sophisticated voice. "One day I came here on a school trip and brought along five miles of dental floss for the saber-toothed tiger. No one ever brushes his teeth."

I could hear a few giggles. I turned and saw kids who had cameras and were obviously tourists.

Bernie was laughing, too. "Now where do you want to go, Courtney?"

I could see the glint in Courtney's sea green, sky blue mysterious eyes.

"Hollywood," she said distinctly.

"Hollywood, it is," Bernie said.

He was a wonderful father. I was beginning to see why Courtney had acted out and been so broken-hearted at the thought of losing Bernie. But it didn't seem as if she had lost him. I felt shocked when a thought hit me—the person he most reminded me of was Howard. Howard wasn't my real father. My father was somewhere here in California, where I was, looking for his big break in the movies.

When we got back to the Rolls, Wilheim Von Dog was yipping and the car phone was ringing. I listened to Bernie talking in this very businesslike way. "Well, this house is a steal at three hundred thousand dollars but if you want something different, we can go down into the Valley. Sure, sweetheart."

Then we were driving again and Courtney was singing "Hooray for Hollywood." She had on her sunglasses and Wilheim Von Dog had on identical little sunglasses.

When I saw it, I gasped. There were the green hills, and at the top huge white letters that spelled out *HOLLYWOOD*.

"They put up that sign in 1923," Bernie said, becoming tour guide again. "It's for starstruck young hopefuls."

I looked over at Courtney, who was smiling. I knew exactly what she was thinking. One day she'd emerge as Tiffany Green, no longer Courtney. She would never be only a young hopeful, she'd make it.

Bernie said he had time for one more spot, and we decided on Mann's Chinese Theater, where all the stars put their handprints in cement. It really did look like a Chinese theater, too. It was in the shape of a big red pagoda.

We all got out of the car, me with my camera, Courtney with Wilheim Von Dog, and Bernie with his cellular phone. He remained at the car, leaning back against it.

All of a sudden I heard this earsplitting scream cut the air.

It was Courtney. "Oh, my God. Look over there. Look who that is!"

I saw a man on all fours with his head almost touching the ground.

"A holy man?" I asked.

"Noooo!" Courtney screeched in her higher-decibel range. "That's Eric Eastman, the movie star. Didn't you see his last picture, *Murder on my Mind?* It was so scary and now there he is putting his handprints in cement. Oh, this is so exciting."

I tried to focus my camera. Felicity and Dawn

would love this. They'd be totally impressed. But there were a lot of people and television cameras around him.

Amidst all the noise and confusion we both heard a distinctive little *clunk.* Wilheim Von Dog's sunglasses had just slipped off. Courtney bent down to get them, and in a flash the little dog leaped out of her arms and ran helter-skelter away from us.

Courtney screeched.

"Wilheim Von Dog!"

It was too late. Just as Eric Eastman was placing his famous hands in the cement, Wilheim Von Dog jumped into the wet, sticky stuff beside him, and Courtney threw herself on top of the dog so he wouldn't run away again. Clutching my camera, I ran over to Courtney, tripped on a piece of TV equipment, and landed on top of her.

Eric Eastman raised his head, and I saw he had very sad eyes for a movie star.

"What do you kids think you're doing?" he said with remarkable restraint.

Courtney, who was in the middle of this human pyramid, said, "Oh, Mr. Eastman, I'm such a fan of yours. I've seen all your movies. My name is Tiffany Green, well it's Courtney, but when I become an actress I'll be changing it to Tiffany. And this is my cousin Cathy." She pointed at me. "She's from New York and she's visiting us for the Christmas holidays."

I could hear a couple of chuckles, but I didn't think anything was very funny. I knew then that the television cameras had been rolling. Out of the corner of my eye, I could just make out Bernie, who was sliding down the Rolls-Royce he was laughing so hard.

I shut my eyes. Even supervised, we had done it again—we had gotten into trouble. Poor Eric Eastman. We had ruined his day in the sun—or cement.

We had to be helped up because we had sunk in so far. Poor little Wilheim Von Dog. There was a kind of *thwunking* sound as we finally pulled him free. Then I saw the slab of cement with six handprints: Eric Eastman's, mine, and Courtney's, four paw prints, and six knee prints, Eric Eastman's, mine, and Courtney's. It was kind of an interesting design. I stood trying to brush the wet, sticky cement off my jeans.

"Will you kids get out of here!" Eric Eastman bellowed. Now everybody was laughing and trying to help Eastman to his feet to help brush him off. The people in charge kept reassuring him that they could level the cement and be ready to start over again in a few minutes.

"Not unless *they're* gone!" he roared.

I wanted to hide somewhere.

"Yes, sir, we're going," Courtney chirped, snuggling Wilheim Von Dog close to her.

I saw Bernie still at the Rolls. He was pounding the top of the silver car with tears streaming down his face.

"Is that your father?" Eric asked me.

"No, sir," I said. "He's my second cousin by marriage."

"Well, that will do."

We all marched over to the Rolls, where Bernie was dabbing his face with a handkerchief.

"This is Eric Eastman, and I think he wants to talk to you, Daddy," Courtney said innocently.

"Aha!" he said. "So she has got a father."

"You know I saw you in *Murder on my Mind,*" Bernie said. "I thought it was your best film."

"Oh?" he said. "You didn't like *Out for Blood,* my vampire movie?"

"We like all your movies, Mr. Eastman," Courtney said boldly. When did she have time to go to school? It seemed Courtney saw every movie that ever came out.

"You know I could sue you for this," Eric Eastman said to Bernie. "Mr.—Mr.—"

"Green," Bernie said. He took out his wallet and pulled out a business card. "Say, I'm in real estate. I can get you a really good deal on a house. Would that help any?"

Eric Eastman cocked his head and shut his right eye. He was really good-looking, tall, blond, with a scar on the left side of his face. I wondered if it was real.

"In Malibu Beach?" he said. "I've always wanted to live in Malibu Beach."

"Sure, call my office in the morning."

They shook hands and someone yelled, "Mr. Eastman, we're ready!" Someone else followed with "Take two!" and there was laughter. I took a picture of Eric Eastman walking away for Felicity and Dawn.

On the way home Bernie was very silent. All at once he pulled the Rolls over to the curb and fell forward on the steering wheel, thumping it as he had another attack of laughing.

I felt like crying because something was whirring in the back of my mind. It was those television cameras. I had the funniest feeling this incident wouldn't be our own little secret.

Chapter Seven

As Bernie drove off and Courtney put her hand on the doorknob beneath the Christmas wreath, Bernice opened the door and said, "Well, you did it again!"

Joan was in the sunken living room looking a lot like a movie star in a pink fuzzy sweater, skinny slacks, and little heels.

"We saw you on the five o'clock news," she said. "Poor Mr. Eastman."

"Did you get it on the VCR?" Courtney asked.

Bernice, who was setting dishes on the dining room table, barely suppressed a laugh. Joan shook her head. "Courtney, Courtney, Courtney."

But I thought of something. I had been in on it, too. My knee prints were also in that cement. I guess she would have been too embarrassed to say, "Cathy, Cathy, Cathy."

"I'm surprised that poor man didn't threaten to sue your father," she said. I bit my lip and started to say something, but Courtney punched me in the arm.

"Okay, kids, I have a surprise for you. There are some pre-Christmas presents under the tree by the pool." Christmas. I had forgotten all about it. I had done all my Christmas cards with carefully hand-printed messages. I had given Felicity and Dawn handmade pins. I had bought Howard a navy tie to perk up his wardrobe. Howard always wore a black suit and black tie to work. And I had saved up to buy my mom a book on animals. It was hard to think of Christmas while you were holding a sack of oranges and grapefruit and enjoying air-conditioning.

Courtney loved surprises and treats. Like a little kid she slid open the doors to the pool and raced out to the glittering Christmas tree.

Once there she stopped and gasped, "Wow! That's super!"

I was speechless.

There were two bikes unlike any I had ever seen. They were bright red, almost neon, with baskets and horns and headlights and handbrakes.

"Cathy, we'll ship yours to New York after you leave," Joan said.

"Oh, super, Joan," I finally said. "Thank you." I was just so shocked. Everything was so grand in Beverly Hills, and the bikes were—super!

Courtney was jumping up and down. "Oh, super, Joan. Super, super!"

"Haven't you ever had a bike, Courtney?" I asked, astonished. It seemed she had everything else. I had had one when I was ten, but it was stolen one day when I was in Central Park.

"No," she said simply. "Everyone drives in Beverly Hills."

"Well, this is healthier," Joan said. "It will get you out of the house, and it will be, uh, better than what you girls have been doing."

I could hear Bernice say behind Joan, "And it will keep you out of trouble." Then she almost choked on a swallowed laugh and went back to setting the table.

We sat down to eat, and I couldn't put Mann's Chinese Theater out of my mind. I sure hoped my mom wouldn't find out. I quickly computed that if the five o'clock news in California had us on it, then that wouldn't hit New York City until eight o'clock. Some rice dribbled off my spoon as I remembered there was always the eleven o'clock news in New York.

The phone rang. It was my mom. She had a knack for beautiful timing. I guess the reason she kept calling was that we had never been separated before except, of course, for the times I went to camp. But this was different. It was like I was halfway around the world.

"Yeah, Mom," I said. "I'm having fun. What did we do today? Well, we went sightseeing with Bernie. Yeah, it was fun. Well, we bought all these oranges and grapefruits and stuff." Pangs of guilt washed over me. I could never keep secrets from my mom. We were very close. Before Howard we only had each other. "And then, Mom, we went to see Mann's Chinese Theater, you know where the stars put their handprints in cement and—"

Before I knew it Courtney materialized right in front of me and whispered loudly, "Cathy, you don't have to tell your mother *everything!*"

"Okay," I whispered back. "Let *me* talk."

"And, Mom, what are you doing? Are you going out tonight? Oh, to a Christmas party—good. No, I mean Christmas parties are good."

She would miss the news. Maybe we wouldn't even be on it.

"Oh, and, Mom, Joan gave us fantastic bikes for a pre-Christmas present."

Courtney nodded her approval.

"Yes, I said thank you. Okay, I miss you, too, and say hello to Howard."

I hung up.

Courtney smiled sweetly at me.

Bernice said, "Have another egg roll, Cathy, while they're still hot."

Joan said, "Girls, I forgot to tell you, Frank called. His grandmother's bringing him over tomorrow. She wants to do some shopping on Rodeo Drive."

Courtney perked up immediately. Why was it I couldn't tell if Courtney liked him or not? Why was it that one minute she acted like she did, and the next minute I was sure she didn't? But what was worse was why it was so impossible for me to just ask. Maybe because if she said she liked him, I'd feel that rejection all over again. What did I know about relationships? That was Courtney's department.

Then I tuned back in to what Joan was saying. "I asked his grandmother if they could rent a bike for him and she said yes."

I smiled, but it was forced. Courtney, Frank, and little me together again. They would talk all the time, and I would feel out of it. My daily entry in my imaginary journal would say—"Stressed out."

That night, as I went to bed, Courtney was softly blowing and popping.

"Cath, are you awake? There's something I wanted to try to tell you if you'll listen."

I didn't answer. I had had enough of getting into trouble. She wanted to know if I was mad at her. I was mad at myself for leaping on top of her at

Mann's Chinese Theater. I was mad at myself because, actually, it had been fun.

The next morning, when we went down to breakfast, Bernice had a picnic lunch all ready.

"Well, this should hold you," she said. "You can put it in the bike baskets."

Courtney was wearing flashy hot pink shorts and a white top tied across her middle. She was dressed a little more sophisticated than she normally was in her T-shirts. Wilheim Von Dog was wearing a bright pink bow, too, of course. Courtney put him in the basket of her bike, and I put the picnic lunch in mine.

Shirley had just come in and said, "Oh, you girls look so cute. Just so cute." I was just wearing jeans and a top, so I figured she must mean Courtney. Enrico Forico was unfastening swatches of material from his shirt and dancing around the room.

Just then the doorbell rang. It was Frank. He said, "I'll be taking driver's education." I immediately understood why he said that. It was because he was embarrassed at being dropped off by his grandmother like a little kid at a birthday party.

"My bike's outside," he said. "Where to?"

By now the whole room was abuzz with activity—the television set always stayed on because Shirley liked to catch the talk shows and news.

"Well," Courtney said, taking the lead. "Why

don't we just get on our bikes and ride. I know a little park near here, and we could have our picnic there!"

I had my camera neatly packed next to the roast beef sandwiches. Great. Now I could have pictures of Frank with Courtney.

Courtney had ridden a friend's bike a few times before. It was a boy's bike, so this was a little different. I hadn't ridden for a while, so Frank helped me, and soon all three of us were pedaling along side-by-side.

The park was farther than Courtney remembered, and it was lunchtime when we got to it. We unpacked roast beef sandwiches and ham and cheese sandwiches and cole slaw and a container of potato salad. There was also a jar of green olives, a thermos of lemonade, and a yummy-looking carrot cake.

Courtney became very silent, engrossed as she was in feeding Wilheim Von Dog a roast beef sandwich. It was very un-Courtney-like. So then Frank and I became very silent, too. I didn't know what to say to Frank, and he never said that much to me when we were alone.

Courtney was having an olive pig-out. She was lying on her back, with Wilheim Von Dog sitting on her stomach, and sucking the pimentos. Her eyes were closed and she seemed blissfully happy.

"How did Howard turn out?" Frank said to me.

"Huh?" I said.

"That guy your mother was seeing?"

"Oh, yeah, Howard. They got married. He's great."

"Tell him about all the stuff you got, Cathy," Courtney coached me.

I blushed. "Courtney! Well, we moved into a big co-op apartment and I got ice-skating lessons and he treated us to a vacation."

"He sounds great," Frank said.

"Do you still have problems with your parents, Frank?" I couldn't believe how bold I was, but it was somehow easier to talk with Courtney there for support.

"Yeah, I'll probably go to my other grandmother's in New York this summer. We can get together." Great. He would be with Courtney, and I would be in the way.

"Tell Cathy about making the junior varsity basketball team," Courtney said over her sucking sounds.

Courtney didn't write—I could attest to that. So I knew she had to be calling him on the phone in her room. I wondered what else she'd found out about him.

Frank poured himself another cup of lemonade from the thermos. "Oh, it was nothing."

Courtney shot up and Wilheim Von Dog yipped.

"Nothing! Your father was really proud of you. That's nothing?"

It wasn't fair. Courtney had Gavin and Rock, but it was Frank she really liked. I felt physically like I was having a heart attack.

Would I ever get over Frank?

Chapter Eight

Courtney sucked the last pimento out of the last olive and tightened the lid on the jar.

"Now where do you want to go?" Courtney asked, placing Wilheim Von Dog, who burped, in her basket as we cleaned up.

"What about just riding around the park on the bridle paths? I love horses," Frank said. "Maybe we'll see some."

Funny, he hadn't said I love anything the summer before.

Courtney rode ahead, pretending she knew the way.

"Are you having fun, Cath?" Frank asked suddenly.

"Oh, yeah," I said. "I've never been out of New York except to go to camp and the time Howard and my mother took me to the Catskills on their honeymoon."

"Oh, that's nice," he said.

"Are you having fun?" I asked. I couldn't believe how relaxed I was. I glanced over at Frank and wondered again how he had a tan already. I decided he was just naturally tan. That lock of golden-sandy brown hair had fallen almost into his amber eyes, and I almost couldn't resist the urge to brush it away. It was just so irresistible.

I wondered if Courtney had the same urge.

Suddenly Courtney squealed, "Oh, my God!" We both looked up sharply, figuring she must have fallen off her bike. But, no, she was still riding. I wondered for a minute if Courtney was into some weird religion. I had read somewhere that people in Beverly Hills were always into new religions.

"What is it, Courtney?" Frank and I yelled.

"It's—it's—it's—"

"Spit it out, Courtney!" I shouted.

"Over there on that horse. That's Bartholomew Barton. Bart Barton—the big movie star who plays in all those action films. I can't believe it. Let's follow him and get his autograph!"

Frank immediately stopped his bike. "Oh, no, I've seen you girls in action. You go ahead. I'm not getting my name in any newspaper. I'll just go back to the pool at your house and turn on the news later tonight to see what you did." He proceeded to turn his bike around and rode off. I gazed wistfully at him. Now I saw what was different. He wasn't just going into ninth grade; he had really gotten older and more mature. We were little girls compared to him, and I wished I could follow him.

"Come on, Cathy, he'll get way ahead of us. He's over there on that horse."

"Which horse?" I saw four horses.

"I have to get his autograph. I have a scrapbook of autographs. I have one hundred and two so far. You can tell a lot about a person by his handwriting."

"You have a scrapbook of autographs, Courtney?" That was so un-Courtney like.

I kept my eyes on the four bobbing figures in riding outfits ahead of us. I could see the deep burgundy behinds and black tails of the beautiful horses.

"Yeah, well, most of the autographs I got through Bernie. I stenciled on the first page of the book: Autographs of Stars."

We had to pedal as fast as we could because the four riders were cantering.

"Which one is he, Courtney?"

"Oh, don't you know? The one in the middle."

There were two middles.

Then one of the middle riders fell off his horse, and the other three just continued ahead.

"Oh, my God!" Courtney shouted. "He fell off his horse, and now he's probably knocked unconscious. Maybe he lost a capped tooth. We have to get to him to help him get on his feet." We pedaled, if it was possible, even faster. But I noticed something then, something out of sync that I would recall later. The horse never left his side. He stayed alert and waiting.

Before we even got close to him, Bart Barton got to his feet, dusted himself off, and mounted his horse by leaping on it from behind. The other three riders had cantered ahead because the whole thing had happened so fast. By the time they returned for him, he was already on his horse.

Courtney cheered. "Hooray! I like a man who can leap back up on his horse. That's real gutsy. That takes guts all right."

It was kind of neat, I had to admit.

"Too bad you didn't get your autograph," I said to Courtney.

"There's always tomorrow," Courtney said.

That was one of Courtney's sayings that usually got us into trouble.

* * *

The next morning I woke early and peeked out through Courtney's white eyelet curtains. I shut my eyes and tried to imagine snow. It was Christmas Eve Day. Christmas Eve was that night.

"Hey, Courtney, wake up!" I said.

"What happened?"

"It's Christmas."

"No, it isn't. If it were Christmas, I'd be getting presents and there'd be a reason to get up early. Go back to bed."

Then, without warning, she shot up and out of bed. "No, get dressed. Today's the day we're going to get Bart Barton's autograph."

"Courtney," I said, practically pleading. "Maybe we shouldn't. We might get into trouble."

"Nonsense," she said dramatically. "Stars love to give out autographs. It helps their egos."

"That guy Eric Eastman wasn't too happy."

"Well, that was different," she assured me. "Besides, Bernie will get his autograph for me."

I looked at the T-shirt she had selected—"HOLLYWOOD." It looked just like those white block letters we had seen in the famous sign on the hill. The letters were kind of bumpy.

"Courtney, do you wear a bra?" I asked.

"Sometimes. But I keep it in the bottom drawer of my dresser. See, this is Beverly Hills. People never walk and they don't wear bras. Do you wear one?"

"Of course." Mine were white cotton with a little rosette in the center. My mom bought them for me.

"Cathy, that thing I asked you about last summer. Do you?"

"Oh, *that* thing. No, any day now. But you probably do. Do you?"

"No, but any day now," she said.

And then we were dressed with Oreos and peanut butter weighing us down. We hopped on our bikes and headed for the special park. Something told me I would rather stay home and splash around in the pool. What if Bart Barton wasn't there? Would Courtney ever quit trying for his autograph?

"I have a special pen for autographs," she said, her voice quiet as it was blown out on the breeze.

I didn't go to action-adventure movies much. I usually went to comedies. I didn't like thrillers or action movies where your heart was hanging in your mouth and you couldn't breath.

Hoping that Bart Barton wouldn't go horseback riding that day, I somehow knew my prayers weren't to be answered. We bicycled along the edge of the bridle path, and all at once Courtney squeaked. It was a small squeak, but it was triumphant. There was Bart just ahead of us. He was riding alone today.

"We'll ride our bikes up to him, and then I'll ask him for his autograph. He should feel important because he hasn't made a movie in a year."

"But what if we scare him and he falls off his horse again?" I asked.

"Trust me, Cathy," she said.

What could I do? I didn't trust her, of course, but it was Christmas Eve Day. All over the country and maybe even the world, people were making last-minute preparations to celebrate Christmas. The least I could do was help Courtney on this day. Somehow I'd rather be home helping my mom get her turkey or ham ready to cook.

"Cathy, can you pedal a little faster? He's getting away!" she yelled, the wind in her mouth.

Probably because he saw us, I wanted to say.

Then we both stopped pedaling and gasped in unison. Oh, no. He had fallen off his horse again in mid-gallop and was lying facedown on the ground like a man sunbathing.

"He's out cold," Courtney said. "We have to rescue him."

"But what if he's in shock?" I said. I had learned all about shock when I was a Girl Scout. "Maybe there's a first-aid station near here."

"C'mon, let's find someone," Courtney said.

We glanced at him as we passed. He was still flat on the ground, his nose pressed into the dirt.

"Maybe he's dead," Courtney said solemnly.

"Courtney, we have to go for help," I said.

We spotted a man picking up trash by stabbing the papers with a long stick with a metal point.

"Sir, there's a man over there. He fell off his horse. It's Bart Barton, the movie star. We think he might be dead," Courtney said.

The man looked over. "Bart Barton, huh? I saw one of his films. Now, which one was it? Let's see. Oh, yes, the one where he leaped across the Grand Canyon holding on to a rope. That was something. But if that's the Bart Barton you're talking about, he just got up onto his horse and is riding away."

We couldn't believe it. He'd done it again—fallen . . . and remounted.

"Maybe horses don't like him," Courtney said feebly.

"Or maybe he doesn't like horses," I said.

"Maybe we should go home," Courtney said, disillusioned.

I put my arm around her as we stood over our bikes. "That's okay, Courtney. There's always tomorrow."

Then, too late, I realized what I was saying and to whom I was saying it.

Chapter Nine

When we finally got home, I was surprised to find the phone wasn't glued to Shirley's ear and that Enrico was wearing a bright red tie on his shirt with all the swatches.

"Grab a cookie and sit down," Enrico said after we washed up.

There was a small platter of little cookies. Some with frosting. Some were little brownies with powdered sugar on top. Some had hard cherries in their centers. I shut my eyes and could see the cookies my mom always baked for Christmas. She cut them out with cutters in the shape of animals. You could smell cookie throughout the apartment while she baked. Afterward she would coat them with egg and sprinkle red and green sugar on their tops.

Courtney must have sensed I was a little homesick.

"Hey, let's open our presents," she said.

"Courtney!" I said, shocked. "You can't do that until Christmas Day. It would ruin all the fun."

"Oh, Cathy, we could open just one apiece. Say, the present I got for you and the present you got for me."

Joan laughed. "Your mother and I used to do that all the time when we were your age. Only it became one more gift and one more until we had them all opened by Christmas Eve."

"Okay," I said to Courtney. "But just one." We shook hands and rushed out to the glittering Christmas tree, shining under the hot Southern California sun. Enrico Forico joined us and sang Christmas carols with his trouser legs rolled up. Dangling his feet in the pool. Shirley danced out with Wilheim Von Dog, who was decorated with red ribbons tied into his curly fur.

"Just one," I said. "Try the one from me to you."

"Just one," Courtney agreed. Her sunglasses were on top of her head like a headband, and I could see her blue-green eyes, her lacy eyelashes, and her rosy nonblushed cheeks. I noticed her Pistachio Pink nails as she lifted a light medium-size box from among all the others. Courtney had the longest nails of anyone I knew. The box said "To Courtney—from Cathy. Love and xxx's." I made every other letter red and the ones in between green.

Courtney ripped off the red bow and shiny gold wrapping paper I had so carefully put on. Then she tore off the top of the fancy white box.

"Oh" was all she said.

"Don't you like it, Courtney?" I asked. Howard had thought of it. It was, literally, a year's supply of gourmet bubble gum. The most exotic flavors ever invented: licorice, cappuccino, lemon mist.

"Bernie gets me these every Christmas," she blurted out.

So that's where she got her never-ending bubble gum supply. I had wondered last summer because she never had to run down to the drugstore.

"Well, maybe we can exchange them for licorice twists or something. I mean I know we can't mail ice cream," I replied. I felt hurt, and when I feel hurt I get a little snippy.

Then she became very perky and said, "Thanks, Cath, for thinking of me," and she kissed me. Which made it worse. "I'll just chain-chew. Or"—and I could see her wheels spinning—"I'll just ask Bernie to buy me a different gift next year since I'll have two this year." She seemed pleased with that. "Now you open yours."

Mine was awfully big. I shook it near my ear, but there was no sound. It was also very, very light. I liked gifts that were mysterious.

"I wrapped it myself," Courtney said proudly. It was a mess. The wrapping paper had "Merry Christmas" printed on it, but there were so many bulges you couldn't even read it. I opened one box and found another box inside. Then I opened another box and found another slightly smaller box inside that. I kept on opening box after box until finally I opened the last small one, and in the middle was a little envelope.

I opened the envelope and saw a gift certificate.

Coiffure Capers for Cathy Bushwick. One haircut and blow-dry. From the Greens.

I could picture my face falling.

"They're open on holidays," Courtney said brightly. "All the stars go there for last-minute touch-ups."

I didn't know what to say. It wasn't that I couldn't say thank you, it was just that I didn't want my hair cut. I liked it the way it was. Most of the time I wore it in a long braid. This was Courtney and Joan's present to me, though, so how could I get out of it and still go home with all my hair?

"Girls," Joan said later after we'd lounged around the pool most of the afternoon. "Why don't you go upstairs and change for dinner. Bernie is stopping by later to take you out for ice cream."

While we were changing, Courtney insisted on putting some makeup on me. Just a little brown eyeshadow and a touch of mascara and some blusher and pretty pink lipstick. She didn't use it. She didn't need it.

When we went downstairs, Enrico Forico blew us wolf whistles. Shirley shook her head from side to side. "Adorable. You girls look adorable."

I was wearing a blue silk dress my mom had bought at Macy's. Courtney was wearing a skirt and blouse in honor of Santa Claus, who would undoubtedly be good to her. Dinner was served by the pool. There was sliced turkey and ham with all the trimmings. Courtney made a Dagwood sandwich out of ham, turkey, coleslaw, and cranberry sauce.

I wondered what it would be like to be as rich as Courtney. I understood a little better why she was the Brat from Beverly Hills. She couldn't help but be a little bratty with all this stuff around.

In the house Christmas carols were playing, and a loudspeaker blasted them over the pool. The sun was just setting. It was kind of pink and lavender. I was having a good time, but worried—how could I tell them I didn't want my hair cut?

I was balancing a plate of food and a glass of eggnog when Frank walked in. I heard Joan say, "Oh, hi, Frank. Don't you look nice. We're having dinner by the pool. Join us."

Suddenly the piece of stuffing I was eating felt like sawdust in my throat, and I had trouble swallowing. I looked up. There was Frank in a gray jacket and white shirt. I didn't want to stare and I couldn't eat. I just moved the pieces of food around my plate.

"Hi, Courtney," he said. She waved a drumstick at him. It was astonishing to see how much Courtney could eat and not gain weight.

He glanced over at me and said, "Gee, you look terrific, Cathy."

I could feel my ears turning pink, which happened whenever I blushed. I was having a wonderful time, but I was also having a terrible time. I'm a person who likes everything clear-cut. Black and white. I feel unsettled, somehow, when things are shades of gray. Also, I was worried. I couldn't figure out Courtney's relationship with Frank. I couldn't figure out how to tell Courtney and Joan I didn't think cutting my hair was a good idea. I just wasn't sure about anything anymore.

After dinner Bernie picked us up and took us all out for ice cream. We went to this huge ice-cream parlor called Crème de la Crème Beverly Hills. Frank had suddenly become quiet and clammed up. I'd seen a lot of boys do the same thing but I had clammed up, too. I was stunned. Everything was so big. The ice-cream sundaes were like two sundaes globbed together. The sodas came in very, very tall frosty glasses. At the next table four people with four spoons were digging into this gigantic banana split.

I was sitting next to Frank, and every time our elbows touched, I felt a little spark of electricity that thrilled me. When you feel that, I always wondered, do both people feel it or is it just one?

It was close to eleven when we pulled up the long driveway to Courtney's house.

"Oh, come on in, Bernie. Joan would love to see you," Courtney said.

Bernie came in reluctantly.

"Doesn't Joan look great?" Courtney said.

I could see what Courtney was trying to do. She was attempting to bring her parents back together even though their divorce was final. Poor kid.

Bernie acted uncomfortable. Joan looked like she wanted him to leave but couldn't say so.

"And we're giving Cathy a haircut for Christmas tomorrow at Coiffure Capers," Courtney said, not leaving one moment's silence. I had forgotten about it for a few hours.

Finally Bernie said "Merry Christmas," and he kissed Courtney and left.

Frank's grandmother was also there to pick up Frank. She was sipping eggnog with Joan.

Finally Frank stood up, kissed Courtney on the

cheek, and wished us all a happy holiday. "Merry Christmas, Cath," he said, taking both my hands and staring into my eyes. Then he dropped his hands very quickly and left with his grandmother. I was stunned. His holding my hands had only lasted a second, but it felt like hours.

Why had he done it?

Chapter Ten

Cathy, Cathy, wake up! It's Christmas Day. Presents!" Courtney said. She was bouncing up and down on my bed. She had been reduced from Beverly Hills sophisticate to seven years old. Maybe six. I looked at her gold-and-red alarm clock shaped like a heart. It was six in the morning. Even for me, who was a morning person, it felt like the middle of the night.

I put on a pink bathrobe, and Courtney just wore her long white nightgown with ruffles. We raced down the steps and dashed out to the pool. The Christmas tree sparkled in the rose-colored sunshine.

Courtney was giggling, picking up different

brightly colored boxes and shaking them to guess what was inside.

Joan had joined us.

Without warning Courtney ripped into the packages and squealed. Wrapping paper and ribbons and perky bows were strewn all over. Mostly she got a lot of clothes, which didn't make sense to me because she already had a lot of clothes.

"Wilheim Von Dog!" Courtney screeched. She woke him up and got him out of his little doghouse. Miraculously he'd spent another night in it.

She found his gift under the tree badly wrapped in shiny red paper. It was a Deluxe Doggie Bone. Confronted with it, Wilheim Von Dog sized it up as if it were another dog. Then he growled and yipped and played with the bone around the edge of the pool while we laughed.

Courtney decided to try on all her clothes at once. She put a bikini top on over her nightgown with white velvet stirrup pants under it and a red silk shirt over it. A baseball cap on her head and white boots on her feet completed the ensemble. She was just deciding what to put on next when Joan handed me a box. "This is from me," she said. Inside was a long-sleeved white cashmere sweater. It was beautiful, better than a fancy white blouse, which I wore a lot. Almost before I had a chance to say thank you, she handed me a box from Bernie. Inside was a book called *I Always Wanted to Be a Writer.*

"Super" was all I could say. Courtney must have told him what I wanted to be.

"Weird to the max!" Courtney said. (She had a funny habit of hanging on to old expressions.) She had been inspecting a mountain of wrapping paper and ribbons.

Joan, who had retired from cooking, decided to make us breakfast since Bernice was off. Even though I wasn't with my mom and Howard, I didn't feel sharp pangs of homesickness. It was turning out to be a wonderful Christmas—until Courtney spoke up once again.

"I know," she said with milk all over her upper lip. "Let's go to Rodeo Drive to Coiffure Capers and watch Cathy get her hair cut. It would look super when she starts back to school, and I bet Phyllis will love it."

Suddenly I felt as if I were going for an operation or facing a firing squad. How could I tell them I didn't want my hair cut? Would they think I was old-fashioned? Weird to the max? Not polite? (Where was my mom when I needed her most?)

We went upstairs to get ready, and I reached into a side pocket of my suitcase, which had been stashed under the bed. "Here, Courtney, these are for you." I counted out twenty-five dollars in unused traveler's checks.

"Oh, Cathy, the bubble gum was enough of a gift," she said.

"No, I mean, it's to pay you back for the haircut. I really don't want my hair cut. Is that enough to pay for the gift certificate? Or did it cost more?" There, I'd done it. Would they hate me forever? Ship me back to New York early?

"Wow! That's super, Cath. You spoke up. You usually have trouble doing that." Courtney logic. No one would ever understand it. "But, Cathy, you don't have to worry about money for the haircut. Why don't you get a manicure instead?"

I couldn't believe it. Maybe that's the way they do it in Beverly Hills. "It's where all the stars go," Courtney assured me. "And they're open every day of the year."

When we got to Rodeo Drive, where Courtney said all the action was, Courtney was beside herself pointing out all the glitzy, glamorous shops. I felt dazed.

As we climbed out of the Rolls, she was holding Wilheim Von Dog, still decked out in red ribbons, and also her autograph book.

The beauty parlor was like a movie set. Everything was pink and bright. I almost needed sunglasses. Courtney had her heart-shaped, red-sequined ones on.

"All the stars come here," she said again. "Look, look over there," she said, nudging me with her elbow as we walked in. I didn't see anyone I recognized.

Then the manicurist came up to us.

I had never had a manicure before, so it was fun.

When it came time to select the nail polish, Courtney squeaked, "Oh, Cath, get Juicy Fruit Red!"

"Pink and Clear," I said firmly.

Just then something or someone had caught Courtney's attention. She had the attention span of a six-month-old infant. Her thought processes whirred very fast.

"Look. Look who that is," she said.

"Courtney, don't point. It isn't nice," I said.

"Oh, they don't mind. She's a movie star or a television star. I just can't remember her name. They all love to be recognized. It's good for their egos."

Courtney boldly went up to the woman, sitting under the hair dryer, and plunged her autograph book down in front of her. The woman glanced at her suspiciously before ducking out of the hair dryer for a moment to sign the book. There were little corkscrews of tin foil in her hair.

"Oh, boy, thank you," Courtney said. "See, this makes one hundred and three."

The woman had reached into her bag for her wallet. "One hundred and three what?" she inquired innocently, opening the billfold.

"Aren't you an actress?" Courtney asked. "A

character actress? Didn't I see you on the Sop-Up paper toweling commercial or as a lady judge on 'The Invisible Witness'? I could have sworn it was you."

"Oh, no, no, I'm Mrs. Stanley Frapp," she said, laughing. "I'm visiting my sister-in-law who insisted I have my hair done today. I live in Grand Rapids, where nothing's open on Christmas Day. I find this whole experience strange. I thought you were selling me a raffle of some sort to help poor children."

We walked away.

Courtney took off her outrageous sunglasses and winked conspiratorially at me. "They like to be incognito," she whispered.

I was beginning to wonder about her autograph book.

After my nails were done, the three of us walked along Rodeo Drive for a while, window shopping, Courtney on the lookout for movie stars. Joan had to remind her that most stars had families and would be at home celebrating. She suggested that's what we should do—go home.

All the way home I couldn't stop staring at my shiny nails. Joan ordered a pizza from the Beverly Hills Deluxe Pizza for the Stars. It had everything on it. Some ingredients I knew and some I didn't know.

Afterward Courtney and I went to sit beside the pool, and while it was warm enough to have a swim, we knew we would have sunk. Instead we sang all the Christmas carols we knew—at the top of our lungs.

I should have known.

Almost on cue, as we were at the height of making fools of ourselves, we heard Joan's voice interrupting us.

"Girls, Frank is here."

Right then I wished I hadn't eaten all the anchovies on the pizza. Anchovies had never really agreed with me. Or was it the butterflies in my stomach? Maybe Frank didn't agree with me. It did seem he was paying more attention to me than to Courtney. Or was that my imagination?

He was wearing a black leather bomber jacket and jeans—and looked totally cool. He was carrying two boxes. Each was wrapped with gold paper and tied with silver ribbons. I knew I would never throw the wrapping paper away. I would carefully place it in my suitcase under some blouses so it wouldn't get wrinkled.

"Super!" I heard Courtney squeal. She had torn into her present like a wrecking crew demolishing a building.

It was a bottle of perfume.

"It's my favorite perfume!" Courtney screeched. How did he know? Or was it really her favorite? With Courtney you never knew what she was wearing. She wore mousse on her hair and scented soap and perfumed nail polish remover and always chewed exotic bubble gum. But Courtney treated every present—except for mine—like someone had given her a million dollars.

"Now, you, Cath," he said.

"Now me?" I repeated like a broken record.

I daintily took the box. My hands were trembling a little, but I could feel it didn't slosh. I liked that. He hadn't gotten us the same thing. Frank had put some thought into his gift giving. I always did.

Gingerly I opened the box. Inside was a very delicate pink-and-white leather-bound notebook. It was lovely. I didn't know what to say. Who else had Courtney told that I wanted to be a writer?

"I can take notes in this," I said stiffly, sounding like an idiot aardvark.

Then Courtney and I lifted out a box for him from under the tree. It was a little hard to find under the avalanche of ripped paper.

"This is for you," Courtney and I said simultaneously, and then paused to stare at each other. We were always going through doors together, too, when we were in a hurry.

Frank studied the box for a while as if determining what it could be. Then, slowly, carefully, cautiously, he removed the red bow and unwrapped the shiny green paper.

"Oh, wow," he said, in an un-Frank-like way, I thought. Courtney had gotten the gift, but we both knew what he wanted.

"The new Raymond Petz," he said, holding the book. "This just came out. I love him." We both knew Frank liked to read detective stories, and Petz was his favorite author.

Then, as if a spell were broken, we could hear Gavin coming through the back of the fence. Rock and his guitar were with him.

"Hi, gorgeous," Gavin said.

Courtney giggled.

For someone who liked everyone, I had to admit I didn't like Gavin. He was too slick even in Beverly Hills, where almost everyone was. Why did he always bring his tennis racket? It was like it was glued to his hand. They came into the pool area and we all sat around while Rock played and sang. Then he switched to Christmas carols, which I thought was lovely.

I was having a terrific time until Gavin picked Courtney up and dumped her into the pool with all her clothes on. Courtney bobbed up giggling and shaking the water out of her curly hair.

That's when I felt homesick. If I were in New York, I would be having a nice cup of cocoa and Howard would have started a fire in the fireplace and my mom would be munching on Christmas cookies.

I also felt sleepy. It's good every day isn't Christmas in Beverly Hills. But, in some ways, I was beginning to think it was.

"Cathy, are you having a good time?" Courtney wanted to know. I was snug under the covers, eyes half open, drowsily watching her brush her curls a hundred times. It was like watching French poodles jump over the pool fence.

I nodded. Not that she could see me.

"Because there's something I think you should know . . ."

Actually, I didn't want to hear this. It would be all about a boyfriend dilemma, and here I couldn't even get one. It's not that I'd ever be really jealous of my cousin Courtney, but she had the one boy I wanted, and she didn't even know or appreciate what she had.

"See, this gets a little complicated, and I know you're not very good with any gray areas in life. Everything has to be black and white."

There she was talking about *my* problems again.

What about the time we accidentally-on-purpose got locked inside Tiffany's jewelry store and we got our knee prints in Mann's Chinese Theater and tried to save a little old man by attempting to bring him cans of sauerkraut but only succeeded in setting off his fire alarm and brought out almost all of Beverly Hills and—

"So I don't know if you'll find this so easy to take, knowing you."

That's the last thing I remember.

When I woke up in the morning, I had forgotten the whole conversation. I would recall it later, though.

CHAPTER ELEVEN

"Cathy, wake up!" Courtney was bouncing up and down on my bed.

"We have to find Bart Barton. Look at what I found," she said.

"It's a book."

"It's more than a book, Cathy, it's the solution to his problem."

"Problem?" I said.

Courtney shoved the book in my face. The title was *Accident-Prone, Fact or Fiction*.

"I found it downstairs on the bookshelf," she said triumphantly. "Before Joan got into the interior-decorating business, she tried to be a talk show hostess. Don't you see, Cath, poor Bart Barton is accident-prone. Maybe there are groups for him like—like 'Klutz, Anonymous' or something. We need to get to him before he hurts himself."

I shook my head. "I don't know, maybe we should leave him alone. Maybe he'll show up in Bernie's office, and you can get your autograph that way. What if he sees us?"

Courtney shrugged. "Cathy, we have a moral duty to save him from himself. One day he's likely to have a fatal accident, and only we can save him from it. He's definitely accident-prone. The book says he likes to be a victim."

"You read the book?" I asked incredulously.

"Not exactly," she said. "I read the book jacket."

I was getting dressed when she added, "He's in real trouble, Cath, and the poor guy doesn't know it. Think of it, we have to save him. We just have to."

I noticed her bright eyes and how excited she was, and for a moment I thought, well, maybe she's right. Then I remembered she was usually wrong.

After breakfast, as we were getting on our bikes, Joan said, "Well, it's nice to see you girls staying out of trouble for a change."

I found myself shuddering, though it was a balmy, Southern California day with a robin's-egg-blue sky and marshmallow clouds. Courtney and I were both wearing jeans, and Courtney had on a Day-Glo environmental T-shirt that said "Earth, I Dig You." We pedaled as fast as we could because Courtney had left Wilheim Von Dog at home and didn't have to worry about his bouncing out of the basket. Courtney said, "With luck he'll be there."

I thought, With luck he won't be there. I didn't only mean lucky for us, I meant lucky for him, too.

We didn't see him riding his horse that day, and also didn't see him picnicking. So far so good, I thought. We could turn around and go home. Then Courtney squeezed her eyes shut as if she were seeing something mystical.

"Courtney, are you all right?" I asked while she was in this trancelike state.

"Yes," she said firmly. "But I wonder if we're in the wrong part of the park. I think there's a big lake here, too. What if he's swimming and has an accident and starts to drown?"

We walked our bikes over to the lake. The lake ended sharply in a waterfall that could have been a descendant of Niagara Falls, which I had never seen, of course. I wished we had brought bathing suits and could just sunbathe and take a dip in the water like normal girls.

"He may be there," Courtney said. "But we have to be very careful. The book says if you sneak up on an accident-prone person, it's like waking up a sleepwalker. It could be dangerous."

"Oh, my God!" she screeched in a voice that would terrify anyone sleepwalking or not. "I think that's him."

I knew what was coming. My stomach was churning. We were going to do it again. Intrude on an innocent person's life.

We left our bikes and raced down the hill to the lake. There was Bart Barton going around in circles on a raft in the water. He was reading a newspaper and smoking a cigar with a Walkman attached to his ears. He was moving perilously close to the waterfall, and there was no one around to tell him to watch out. He was oblivious to what was just ahead—the falls. He was going to be killed. It was terrible!

Courtney jumped into the water with all her clothes on except her shoes. "Come on, Cathy, he'll drown!"

For a moment I stalled. I didn't know what to do. Finally I said, "I'm not such a good swimmer," held my nose and jumped in.

Courtney said, "That's okay, it's only up to your neck in places." All through this Mr. Barton never noticed us. He was still reading his newspaper and listening to his Walkman, oblivious that the falls were yards away. He must have had the music cranked way up in volume.

"Oh, my God!" Courtney yelled. "He's going over the falls in that raft. Mr. Barton! Sir! Keep swimming, Cathy. We have to let him know there are therapy groups for people like him."

I was dog-paddling now, and tears were rolling down my wet face. Too bad he wasn't in trouble on the ice-skating rink. Then I knew I could help him.

"Come on, Cathy!" Courtney yelled while she swam. "Come on, Cathy, he's getting nearer and nearer the falls. Yell with me—'Please, Mr. Barton, come back!' "

Water was clogging my nose now. I tried to yell, but I was swallowing too much water as I tried to gulp in air. I decided we were trying to save the wrong person. I was the one who was going to drown. I vowed then if Howard ever offered me more lessons, I'd ask for swimming lessons. I managed a garbled, "Please, Mr. Barton, come back!"

My head went under, and every time I bobbed up to gulp air I gulped more water. Then I could hear Courtney moaning over and over, "Oh, no, oh, no."

At that point Courtney swam over to me and helped to keep me afloat. "It's too late," I heard her saying when my head was out of the water long enough to hear. "It's all over. And to think we tried so hard."

Courtney dragged me out of the lake and pushed me down and proceeded to sit on top of me until I spit out water. As soon as I could get her off me, we ran over to check the bottom part of the falls.

"He might as well have gone over Niagara Falls in a barrel," Courtney said.

We stared forlornly at his raft floating around in the water. His hat wasn't far away. His soggy newspaper, like the remnant from a shipwreck, was plastered against a rock.

"I feel like crying," Courtney said. I realized that I had never seen Courtney cry.

"I do, too," I said. "We should tell the authorities what's happened."

"They'll want to take the body to the morgue," she said sadly. I sighed deeply. It was so sad. For once Courtney had been right—he was accident-prone, and we could have saved his life.

We left our bikes and ran up to the top of the falls. We found a police officer standing in front of an ice-cream stand. Courtney spoke first.

"A movie star is dead," she said.

"A real movie star?" he asked.

"Yes, yes! Bart Barton. He drowned just now."

I could see the officer wasn't taking us seriously.

"Was it homicide or suicide?" he asked.

"It was an accident," Courtney said. "See he's accident-prone and we came down here today to let him know and save his life and now it's too late and he's gone and I didn't even get my autograph."

The officer patted Courtney's arm. He finally believed us and radioed for an ambulance. "They should be here soon."

We were standing there in dripping wet clothes. "We tried to save him," Courtney explained. "But he couldn't hear us with his Walkman on. He just went over the falls in a raft."

We walked back with the officer to where we had left our bikes. I tried to wring out my jeans as I heard the sirens in the background. That was probably the ambulance and more police.

"Where do you girls live?" he asked us.

"My name is Courtney Green," Courtney said, "no *e* at the end, and I live in Beverly, like the girl's name, Hills, California."

Then he turned to me. I gulped. Would they have to file a report? Probably they would and we would be waiting in the police station forever. This time Bernice wouldn't be laughing. Maybe it was our fault this Bart Barton was dead. Maybe he rolled over the falls just to get away from us.

Choking back a sob, I said, "Cathy Bushwick, New York City, New York."

"What relationship did you have with the deceased," he asked us.

"None," I said.

"Fans," Courtney said.

I could see the ambulance and a crowd forming. People must have seen the police officer and guessed where the ambulance was going. As they approached they were saying things like—"Who's hurt?" "Does anyone know?" and "Someone must have had a heart attack."

I thought *I* was going to have a heart attack. Bart Barton was a famous star. It would be on all the radio and TV programs. He was found by two girls. Please, God, I prayed, don't say two *little* girls.

The ambulance had gotten there in record-breaking time, and Courtney was telling our story. "Then I found this book—*Accident-Prone, Fact or Fantasy,* and I knew we had to save his life. It's just that we were too late."

I could hear more sirens, and I knew it had to be the Beverly Hills police.

When they arrived, one of them said, "Weren't you those two little girls who were involved in that breaking and entering at the Museum for Silent Films?"

I tried desperately to straighten out my clothes, but they were clinging to me like a transparent bathing suit. Everyone was talking at once when one police officer said, "Hey, is that the guy you mean?"

We peered across the lake far from the falls. Courtney almost fell over. I gasped as if I'd seen a ghost. There was Bart Barton reclining on his raft, reading his soggy paper, earphones in place—the Walkman must be one of those waterproof kind. He was just floating around aimlessly. I couldn't believe it!

"Hey, there, you on the raft, come ashore!" The police officer shouted into a bullhorn. Then he blew a whistle. That got Bart's attention.

Bart Barton, acting very confused, squinted at the police and paddled ashore. The police threw out a rope, and he was towed the last bit before he climbed onto the grassy bank. "Has there been an accident, officers?"

"You're supposed to be dead, Mr. Barton," one of the officers said.

He gazed around at the squad car and the crowd and the ambulance and said apologetically, "I'm not."

"But you went over the rapids before we could save you!" Courtney cried. "And you're supposed to be dead. You disappeared for a long time."

"I'm sorry," he said again, and I wondered why he was apologizing. Here it comes, I thought. I wondered what it would be this time. What logical, realistic answer to sink Courtney.

"Are you Bart Barton, the movie star?" the officer asked.

Courtney took out her sopping-wet autograph book from her jeans pocket and said in a small voice, "Does anyone have a waterproof pen."

Bart Barton started to laugh. "Oh, now I get it.

You thought I was him." He laughed some more, holding his sides. "You thought he was me. That's the funniest thing I ever heard." Now he was laughing so hard he was all doubled over, and an officer had to help him to stand up. After all, he *had* gone over the falls in a raft.

Chapter Twelve

The officer gave him a handkerchief to blow his nose.

"This is priceless," he said. "You see, I'm not even Bart Barton, and I'm definitely not dead."

"You're not Bart Barton?" someone from the crowd said. "But you look just like him."

He was still laughing. "No, I'm his double. His stuntman. We do look alike, but if you really look closely you can see that I'm not. My name is Derek Derek and I come here to practice stunts so I stay in shape."

"You mean he doesn't do his own stunts?" a man from the crowd said loudly.

"Not anymore. He can't. He's insured for a million dollars now that he's a top star."

"You mean he didn't fall off a roof and roll around on the ground while he shot the other guy?" someone said.

"No, I did that. The camera wasn't on a close-up, if you remember."

"And he didn't leap over the Grand Canyon on a rope?" someone else said.

Derek Derek shook his head. "No, I did that," he said.

I began to get the idea. "So you went over the falls in a raft. But why?"

"I couldn't find a barrel," Derek Derek said with a twinkle.

I could see that Courtney was somehow disappointed. The man had come back to life, and he wasn't the real Bart Barton. She wanted to get his autograph. I felt humiliated. To think we did this because we thought he was accident-prone and needed psychiatric assistance. Well, at least no one knew what we thought.

Someone gave Derek a match to light his soggy cigar. "Actually this is good. No, this is good. I sure can use some publicity, and this is a great story. Say, do you know if there's a phone around here? I have to make a call."

I squeezed my eyes shut. He had to make a call,

but it wasn't to his attorney. It wasn't to his barber. Nor to his mother. It was to his publicist. This was how they'd break the news to the world that he did Bart Barton's stunts.

Courtney was trying to wring the water out of the legs of her jeans. When that proved useless, she finger-combed her wet curls.

"Well, you can call from the police station," the officer said. "We'll have to make out a report because you're supposed to be dead. It'll probably only take an hour or two."

An hour or two while reporters came and we got on TV again. Courtney would have drip-dried by then, and she would be at her best. All I could think was that Joan would be so frantic with worry she'd call the Missing Persons Bureau before she called my mom in New York.

Anyway, we did end up going to the Beverly Hills Police Station with the cops carrying our bikes in another squad car. At the station Courtney went right into her routine. "My name is Courtney Green, no *e* at the end. I'm from Beverly, like the girl's name, Hills, California, and this is my cousin, Cathy, who's visiting from New York for the Christmas holidays." I turned around so I wouldn't have to face the camera. I guess the cameraperson just got a shot of my damp braid hanging down my back.

Derek Derek acted like the whole incident was

one great big birthday party in his honor. Courtney was charming the reporters while I imagined taking a giant eraser and erasing myself.

Joan rushed into the room near tears, and Bernie, talking to one of the officers, seemed to be on the verge of crying, too, but I knew he was laughing. I knew someone would have called them. It was just a matter of time.

Joan went up to Derek Derek and said, "Oh, Mr. Derek, I'm so sorry about the girls bothering you."

"Oh, no problem. I get all this nice, free publicity. It was about time. Jay Leno's invited me on his talk show. You know, this is how Bert Reynolds got started."

"And don't forget the autograph," Courtney said. Derek Derek had promised her Bart Barton's autograph.

Then, thankfully, the three-ring circus was over, and we went home and changed into fresh clothes even though our wet clothes had dried by then. This time Bernice had the VCR on as they played our story at the very end of the news, the time reserved for human interest stories. There was Courtney smiling into the camera, and there was my long braid hanging down my back.

The last days of my vacation were the best part. First because we managed to stay out of trouble, and that was the most comfortable for me—being a good girl. Also, Courtney and I got a chance to talk, really talk, when all the boys weren't around. Gavin came over. Rock came over. Some other boys from Courtney's class came over.

Of course, usually what Courtney talked about was boys.

That's what we were doing that day by the pool.

"When you stop to think about it, Cath, there's not too much difference between boys and girls."

That's funny. I always thought there was.

"See, boys just act different sometimes. A lot of boys are shy and they act like they're not."

"Like who?" I asked. The only boy I thought was shy was Frank. He was shy and he acted like it sometimes. But that was my opinion.

"Gavin is basically shy," she announced. I couldn't believe that. "Oh, yes," she said as if she could read what I was thinking. "See, that's why he always travels with his tennis racket. It's a prop."

"He probably takes it to bed with him."

Courtney laughed.

I wasn't used to Courtney laughing at my jokes.

"Now, take Frank, for instance. Frank is basically shy, too." So she noticed. That matched my theory of opposites attracting. But Frank must know that Courtney had a few boyfriends. Boys just naturally gravitated to her.

"Remember, Cath, if a boy is down to his last dollar or his allowance has been cut off, let him buy you a candy bar."

That didn't make any sense to me. Besides, I hardly ever ate candy bars. That would mean I'd get cavities and have to go to the dentist, and we had always been so poor.

"And another thing about boys," she said, popping a bubble, "is that you have to compliment them a lot. Most of the time they have little egos, but they won't admit it."

I wondered how she complimented Frank. Did she say—you're gorgeous? Sensitive? Athletic? Kind? Courtney didn't know how lucky she was.

"But I really have to tell you something about Frank. See, I've been trying to do it, but—"

She blew a bubble then, and it burst, covering her face. As she was peeling off a mass of orange icky stuff, we heard Shirley scream. Sometimes she worked outside in a bathing suit with a cellular phone.

Joan came rushing out. We all turned to Shirley to see what was wrong.

Shirley covered the phone with her hand. "It's New York. They want to talk to Ms. Green about a movie."

"Oh, I've never done clothes for a movie. This is fabulous!" We all watched as Joan took the phone.

"Yes, this is Ms. Green. Oh, I see. No, I'm her mother. You want Ms. Courtney Green? She's my daughter. Yes, she's here."

Courtney ran over to Joan, who handed her the phone.

"Yes, this is me," she said. "Uh-huh, uh-huh. Yep. Sure, uh-huh, uh-huh."

Courtney's hand was over her mouth, and she was screaming and jumping up and down as if she'd won an Academy Award. "Yes, oh, yes, but wait, you better ask my mother, I mean, Joan," she said.

Joan got on the phone and listened for a long time, and then she finally said, "Yes, but you'd better ask Bernie—her father, I mean." Then she gave New York Bernie's number.

Courtney was still jumping up and down and speaking totally incoherently. We couldn't tell what she was saying. Finally she just jumped into the pool. I could see her blue-green bikini as it darted along creating waves. Wilheim Von Dog, who was wearing a green-and-blue bow, started to whimper. Courtney got out, dried her hair with a towel, and picked up Wilheim Von Dog.

"I got a movie," she said as if she had been acting for years. "Remember Clint Carothers from last summer, the soap opera star who went on to Broadway in *The Laundry Bag Murder?*"

Remember? How could I forget. I never got to see

the show, but I read the reviews. They said the show was . . . "bubbly!"

"Well, they're making a movie of the play, and Clint Carothers is not only starring in it, he's directing it, and your mom sent him one of my eight-by-tens. He recognized the picture, and I don't even have to audition or anything because they wrote my part in. It's exactly what we did last summer. I discover the murder." She put a fresh piece of bubble gum in her mouth.

"That's great," I said, feeling genuinely excited for her. What an opportunity to be a movie star. "When do you leave?"

"I get to finish out the school year because they won't start until the beginning of the summer."

"You can stay with us!" Now it was my turn to jump up and down. "Can you wear your sunglasses?"

"He didn't say."

"Can you chew bubble gum?"

"He didn't say."

"So you and I will be together again this summer. I guess I'll go back to Camp Acorn as a counselor." Frank would be there. I guess I was also thinking that if she was working all day, we could stay out of trouble. There would be no more Courtney escapades.

She picked up Wilheim Von Dog and hugged him and suddenly became very pensive. Especially for a Courtney who had just been given a part in a movie, her dream come true.

"Look, Cath, I think Frank likes you," she blurted out.

"He likes you," I said almost stubbornly.

"We're friends," she said, shrugging.

"So what does that mean?"

"Well, basically," she said, popping a bubble, "it means you're shy and he's shy and I wanted to tell you all along but you wouldn't listen and I knew if you listened you'd have a heart attack."

Instead of being elated by the news, I somehow felt deflated like a balloon that's whizzing around the room getting smaller and smaller and suddenly plops on the floor, just a little piece of flat rubber.

I didn't know what to think, what to do, what to say. Was she trying to tell me Frank wanted more than one girlfriend? Was I . . . the Other Woman? No, I actually think she meant what she said. I would never forget her saying, "I think Frank likes you." I could write it in my diary when I went home.

But this was all so confusing.

I needed to be alone to think this out.

That's just the way I am.

Chapter Thirteen

On my second-to-last day Bernie came over to say goodbye. I found myself flinging my arms around him while he kissed me on the top of my forehead.

When Courtney was helping me pack, she said, "Did you notice how Bernie looked at Joan? Maybe they'll get together again."

I put down the top I was folding and said, "Courtney, your problem is you're not realistic. They're not even remotely comfortable with each other. Bernie is happy. Joan is doing her own thing. She has Enrico Forico and Shirley. Life doesn't always give you a happy ending."

I was trying to push what she had said about Frank to the back of my mind because it had confused me.

Courtney looked sad.

She loved happy endings. I knew that, but I felt I had to say something before she got her hopes up. I knew I felt the same way about my dad when he left. I kept thinking—maybe he'll come back one day.

Almost to my surprise I rolled up two socks and pitched them angrily into my suitcase.

Courtney almost swallowed her bubble gum.

"Cathy, you know what you just did? You just had a temper tantrum."

"I did?" I stared at my socks.

"Yes. What I told you about Frank. All your emotions are globbed up inside like a stale piece of bubble gum, and they're gumming up the works."

More armchair psychology, but maybe she was right. I didn't know how I felt about what she'd said.

"But, Cathy, yours *is* a happy ending. He likes *you*—not me. I've been trying to tell you since the first day you came."

I kept packing and even picked up speed. "Well, first of all," I interjected. "Why didn't he tell me himself?"

"I think he tried to tell you, but he's too shy. I told you boys can't talk as well as girls. Besides, he thought you had eyes and would figure it out."

Eyes. The long walk down the driveway. The picnic. The Christmas gift that was special for me. The flirting elbows at the ice cream parlor—eyes.

How come I never saw what other people saw?

"Your problem is you're *too* realistic. Sometimes there are happy endings." I wondered how much she and Frank had talked about this behind my back. Courtney was chain-chewing. She did that when she got nervous. A used glob of strawberry bubble gum was on the back of her hand while she blew a big, blue bubble that popped all over her face. She was chewing Bluesberry now.

"Listen, Cath, boys are weird. He didn't know he liked you. Well, he did like you first and then he thought he liked me, but then he realized he really did like you and not me and he'd made a mistake. And Frank can't cheat. Don't forget your cutoffs."

Now I was packing mindlessly, tossing things helter-skelter when I was usually so painstakingly careful.

"Okay, I think I understand," I finally said. "But I hate hand-me-downs, which is what Frank is. See, even when we were very poor, I would never take hand-me-downs."

Courtney put the Bluesberry blob of gum on the back of her hand and took a piece of licorice bubble gum. I watched as her teeth and tongue turned black.

"Cathy," she pleaded. "He's not a hand-me-down.

He's a boy. And he likes you. He told me when we came back to Los Angeles at the end of the summer. But what could I say? See, boys can't always identify their emotions. They're like underdeveloped girls. Don't forget the two white blouses hanging in the closet. Now take me. I'm off boys. Joan is taking me to the library, and I'm going to fill up the Rolls with books on acting."

"No more boys?" I asked increduously.

"Nope."

"Impossible," I replied, folding a top. "What about the hunk—Gavin?"

"Weird to the max," she said, dismissing him with a wave of her hand. "He's too slick. He loves himself first and his tennis racket second and sometimes he gets the two confused."

I laughed. So she had seen what I had seen. But I wondered if she would still hang with Gavin, just to have a boy around.

"I'm off boys," she said seriously.

"Yeah, sure, in the year 2004, when you're all grown up and married and a famous movie star, you'll be off boys."

Courtney took a pillow and wound up with it like a pitcher. Then she smacked me on the head.

I ran around to the other twin bed, took a pillow, and whacked her. We were both laughing. Then we pounded each other with the pillows at the same time and fell all over the bed laughing and gasping until I couldn't catch my breath. Courtney's face was as orange as her hair, and she was laughing so hard she was crying.

Suddenly the door opened and there was Joan.

"Cathy, Frank is here to see you."

Courtney smacked me on the back a few times until I had calmed down and was breathing.

"Coming, Courtney?" I asked.

"No, Cath," she said. "He's here to see you."

"What should I wear?"

Everything was packed. My dress for the plane was hanging in the closet. All I had were the jeans and shirt that I had on. My long braid was coming out but there was no time to redo it. I didn't even have shoes on. Frank was downstairs and I knew he liked me and it was all right to go downstairs barefoot.

"It's okay, Cath. You look great. You could look like Godzilla. He likes you."

That made me feel even better.

Until I thought about it.

"Here, put a slash of Juicy Orange lipstick on," Courtney said.

Why was Frank here?

Slowly I walked down the white-carpeted movie-star stairs wishing with all my heart that my cousin Courtney could come with me for support. Then I thought about Frank. No matter what he had to say, it must be hard for him to say it. Frank never said much, but I knew we were a lot alike.

He was out by the pool sitting on a chaise lounge. I prayed I wouldn't trip. His sandy-colored hair was sun-bleached now with flecks of gold. His sunglasses were resting on top of his head.

I noticed Shirley had left the pool, Enrico Forico, too. Joan was busy elsewhere, and I figured Courtney was at her window with a pair of binoculars.

"Hi, Cath," he said.

"Hi, Frank," I said, sitting down on a chaise lounge next to his.

Then neither of us said anything.

"Did your grandmother bring you?" I asked.

Oh, no, how dumb. He couldn't have walked from Burbank.

"Yeah, she's waiting outside in the car."

I hoped she had a radio, because this looked like it might take a while.

"The thing of it is, Cath, last summer—"

"Yes, Frank?"

It seemed like he couldn't continue.

I guess he didn't want to say what I already knew.

He started over.

"This summer I'll be working as a camp counselor at Camp Acorn. Will you be there? I'd like us to be together. As boyfriend and girlfriend."

My blood pressure soared and I could feel a smile spread all across my face until I must have looked like a little kid.

Frank was smiling, too, as he took my hands in his. They felt very warm and secure.

"Will you write to me, Cathy?" he asked. "Courtney has my address."

"Courtney wrote you a letter?"

"No, but she has my address."

Then he stood and was shaking my hand.

"Well, my plane leaves early tomorrow morning. It's not so long to wait until summer vacation."

Yes, it is, I thought. It was an eternity. He was my first boyfriend, and he was ABSOLUTELY GORGEOUS.

When I got upstairs, Courtney was sitting on the bed.

"Well?" she said, jumping up and down.

"Well," I said. Well, actually, Frank hadn't said much. He never said much. But what he said was good enough to last me until spring vacation and carry me to June.

"So you have a boyfriend," Courtney said. Then she whispered under her breath, smugly, "There *are* happy endings."

I hated to go, but the next afternoon Joan and Courtney drove me to the airport. We kissed and hugged goodbye. I had souvenirs, a bag of oranges and grapefruits, and my Christmas presents and an inability to concentrate because now I had a boyfriend and I was in love.

I wondered if this would affect my grades in school.

I always tried for all A's and studied very hard.

Then I realized something.

We had been so busy getting into trouble and celebrating Christmas and convincing me that Frank liked me that I had forgotten to read Courtney anything out of my book about her.

Or maybe I was shy.

Oh, well, I had to revise it. I had to allow for the next summer when Frank came and Courtney became a movie star and it was back to Camp Acorn. Sitting on the plane, thinking of my vacation, I took out the pink-and-white notebook Frank had given me and opened it to the fresh first white page. Then I began to print.

I drew flowers and hearts around the word *Tiffany,* which was Courtney's stage name. I couldn't believe she'd be a thirteen-year-old movie star even though I knew she'd been rehearsing for the part all her life. I drew circles of throbbing hearts around the names *Frank* and *Cathy*. This was too good to be true. Wait until I told my mom!

Then, as if my hand had a will of its own, I wrote

in big, block letters, MY CRAZY COUSIN COURTNEY RETURNS AGAIN!

This time as a movie star. As I stared into a cloud, I knew there would finally be a way to keep my crazy cousin Courtney out of trouble! But then, I drew a big question mark and stared at it.

Movie stars didn't get into trouble—did they?

About the Author

JUDI MILLER was brought up in Cleveland, Ohio, but writes and lives in New York City. She is the author of *My Crazy Cousin Courtney* and *My Crazy Cousin Courtney Comes Back,* both available from Minstrel Books. The third book in the series about Cathy and her cousin Courtney will be *My Crazy Cousin Returns Again.* Judi, who has liked to write since she was nine years old, also writes suspense thrillers for adults.